SEE ME

Breaking the Rules Series

H.R. Hobbs

ISBN 978-0-9953448-0-8

To Terry, for all the love and support, always.

TABLE OF CONTENTS

CHAPTER ONE

*N*o! No! No! Not behind me. Anywhere but behind me, I thought to myself, keeping my eyes firmly on my desk, trying to be invisible. My shoulders lifted and I tucked my chin to my chest to make myself as small as possible. *Disappear,* I thought, *don't let them see you.*

Mrs. Barkowski stood at the front of the room with what appeared to be our newest classmate. I quickly glanced over Alex's shoulder and saw him standing in front of Mrs. Barkowski's desk, shifting his weight from one foot to the other as if he had to pee. His dirty blond hair was cut short on the sides, the top longer and hanging over one eye. He was dressed in worn jeans and a T-shirt with Darth Vader on it. Both had seen better days. Mrs. Barkowski's hand crept like a claw around his shoulders, making him appear even more uncomfortable. His body stiffened like a board and he eyed her hand distastefully. I could tell he didn't like people touching him. Strange.

Mrs. Barkowski appeared oblivious to his reaction as she introduced him to the class.

"Class, this is our newest member, Toby Cavanagh. Toby has just moved here from Leduc. Please be sure to show him around and make him feel welcome."

Twenty-four sets of eyes stared at Toby—all but mine. I kept my eyes firmly planted on my math notebook in front of me, and I imagined myself sinking through the floor.

I heard Toby say to Mrs. Barkowski, "Call me Chip."

"Why would I call you that?" Mrs. Barkowski said, and I looked up despite myself. Her fists sat on her ample hips and her eyebrows disappeared into her curly brown bangs.

"That's what everyone calls me," he replied, a look of determination on his face.

This wasn't going to go well, I could tell.

Mrs. Barkowski's face mirrored Toby's, staring right back at him. "Well, Toby, in this class we go by our given names. You may take the seat behind Hannah."

So much for being invisible.

"Awesome," Toby mumbled, in a way that said he didn't think it was awesome at all. He moved down the aisle with his hands in his pockets and his feet scuffing the worn linoleum floor. He sat down behind me and I knew he was slouched in his seat because I felt his feet make contact with mine underneath my desk. I immediately moved my own feet forward.

"All right, class, let's turn to page forty-three of our textbooks and look at multiplication of decimals," Mrs. Barkowski instructed.

A textbook suddenly appeared before me and I looked up to see the back of Alex's large, brown head with his hand behind it holding a textbook. He gave it a shake and I realized he wanted me to take it—it must have been for Toby. I took it and passed it to him.

"Thanks," he muttered, opening it.

Mrs. Barkowski began her lesson on multiplying decimals, writing examples on the board that we diligently copied into our notebooks and solved. We were on the fourth example when I felt a finger poke between my shoulder blades. I didn't move.

A few seconds later, there was another poke, harder this time, and a whispered "Hey."

Still I faced forward and tried to concentrate on the next example—both basic tactics for staying invisible in the seventh grade.

The third poke to my back came with a "You got a pencil and a piece of paper?" from behind me. This was a little louder than the first "Hey," and a couple of my classmates seated close to us sent disapproving glances in our direction.

As quietly as possible, I took a spare pencil from my pencil case and a piece of paper from my notebook and handed them back over my shoulder.

"Thanks," Toby muttered again.

Five minutes later, Mrs. Barkowski gave us our assignment and the class began working quietly.

Again a poke to my back, this time with a pencil.

"What's your name?" came from behind me.

I ignored it and continued working on question number four.

"Hey, tell me your name."

Out of the corner of my eye, I could see Trudy Hartford give us both a look that clearly said, "You're disturbing me and my brilliance, quit talking so I can get my work done." Her contemptuous look made me uncomfortable. The hairs on the back of my neck stood up and my face heated with a flush of red. She continued to stare for a moment and then flicked her brown, shiny hair over her shoulder and bent her head back to her book.

I quickly turned in my seat before he could poke me in the back or talk again and hissed, as quietly as possible, "It's Hannah. Now do your work and leave me alone!"

"I'm done," he replied.

I stared at him. His brown eyes met mine and he tilted his head at the same time, quirking up one eyebrow.

"What?" he said.

"You're done? How is that possible? Mrs. Barkowski assigned us twenty questions barely five minutes ago," I whispered incredulously.

"They were easy and math is kinda my thing, so it only took me a couple of minutes," he said, louder yet, and shrugged his skinny shoulders.

"Look, I'm glad you're done, but I'm not and Mrs. Barkowski does not tolerate any talking during work time, so save us both from getting in trouble and be quiet!"

Toby looked down at his paper. I whirled around to face forward in my desk, hopeful that he'd take my advice. I didn't hear another sound out of him for the rest of the class.

When the bell rang, Toby followed me out of the classroom. I turned right and headed down the hallway to the stairs. I could sense him behind me and I quickened my steps, my sneakers slapping the floor, to avoid any more conversation. I liked to be invisible at school and having the new boy in class talk to me would draw attention that I didn't want—no one here saw me and that was how I wanted it to stay. He didn't know this, but right now I didn't have the time or patience to fill him in. I nearly made it to the stairs when a hand touched my arm. I froze.

"Hannah, my next class is Science. Can you tell me where the lab is?"

I looked at Chip's fingers on my arm and weighed the pros and cons of helping him. On the pro side, he might leave me alone once I helped him. On the con side, he might see it as encouraging—and then I'd never get rid of him. I sighed. The lesser of two evils was to help him now and ditch him at the first opportunity.

"I'm headed there. Follow me," I said without looking at him.

As we made our way down the stairway to the next floor, Toby walked beside me calling out and waving to various students: "Hey, how's it goin'?" or "Hi!" I kept my head down and powerwalked to the end of the hallway, turning left into the science lab.

As I passed Trudy filing her nails at the front bench I heard her stage-whisper to Anne, her lab partner, "Looks like Hannah has a new friend."

Anne snorted and said, "Well, at least she has one," and they both collapsed into giggles.

Toby heard the comment and quickly replied: "Yep, and that's all she needs."

As I made my way to the bench at the back of the room, Toby followed me and plopped himself down beside me.

"Thanks," I said, "but you didn't have to do that."

"Oh, yes, I did."

"Why?"

"Well, I know I need a friend if I'm going to make it here, and it looks like you do, too." He stuck out his hand. "Let's start over," he said. "I'm Chip. Nice to meet you."

I studied his hand in front of me and then slowly reached up and grasped it.

"Hi, Chip. I'm Hannah." As our hands moved up and down, I glanced up to find a goofy grin pasted on Chip's face.

* * *

Later that night, I sat cross-legged on my bed, my writing note-book open in my lap. I flipped through the pages of journal entries, poems, and drawings until I got to a blank page. I scribbled today's date at the top and then tapped the pencil to my lips, thinking.

I thought about Chip … the way he stood up to Mrs. Barkowski, his friendly way of greeting strangers, and his irritating ability to get math done in ten minutes. I noted all these qualities in my notebook. The most disturbing was his observation that I needed a friend and his determination that it be him. I didn't need a friend, I got by just fine on my own—unfortunately, I doubted Chip saw it this way.

I closed my book, returned it to my backpack, and flopped back onto my bed to stare at the ceiling.

Yep, he was going to be trouble.

CHAPTER TWO

I wasn't always invisible. There was a picture of me, age two, that sat on the shelf next to my grandmother's chair. I had fine, white blond hair that curled around my head. My bright blue eyes were full of laughter and my smile showed every one of my pearly white teeth. There was a look of joy on my face. Once, my light shone as bright as the sun.

The picture was taken before I started to disappear. But now I didn't let people see my light anymore, I kept it hidden. And I knew the exact moment that my light started to dim.

I'd lived in the same house, on the same street, for all of my thirteen years. I lived with my parents, Lorraine and Mike, on the corner of Prescott Ave and First Street in a small, white bungalow surrounded by lilacs with two giant evergreens out front. Across the street was the elementary school. A two-storey brick building with wide steps leading to the front door.

Acadia was your typical small town: two grocery stores, three gas stations, and not much else. Prescott Ave was your typical small-town street. There were the McNevins next door, who owned one of the grocery stores. Mr. and Mrs. Patrick lived a couple of doors down. Mr. Patrick was the manager at the local bank. Right in the middle of the block lived my grandparents: Steve and Eve. Yeah, their names rhymed, and that was just about their only similarity. My grandma was a feisty woman who was set in her ways and didn't take crap from anyone, especially my grandpa. Grandpa Steve was a big guy with a loud laugh, who loved to play practical jokes. This usually earned him a dirty look from Grandma on most occasions and a good talking to on others.

I knew everyone on my street and when I was little that block was the center of my world. I had a routine: stop and check out the pine cones that fell from the two giant evergreens in my front yard. Stop to pet Herman, the McNevins' cat, as it soaked up the sun on their front step, or visit with Mr. McNevin while he washed his car on Sunday. Working my way up the block, I would pick some petunias for my grandma from Mrs. Patrick's flower bed (if she wasn't looking out the window). Finally, I would arrive at my grandma's house, where we'd bake cookies, or have some cinnamon toast if it was still early in the morning. As long as I stayed on my block, my parents weren't too concerned about me when I left the house, safe in the knowledge that there were people who looked out for me. My days were carefree … until I learned that there were rules you didn't break.

Part of my light was my curiosity. One day, when I was four, I ventured down the back alley behind my house, intending to visit Grandma, when I met Suzy, who lived on the next block. I had never met Suzy before. I was the only child that lived on my block, so someone my own age was a novelty. Suzy invited me to her house—I was so excited to have a friend my own age!

It wasn't until sometime later, as we were swinging on the swings in Suzy's backyard and my dad found me, that I realized that I had broken the rules. He entered the yard with a dark look in his eyes I had never seen before and grabbed my hand off the swing. I was confused. I didn't understand why he was acting this way, but I said nothing, petrified of this version of my dad I'd never seen before. He didn't let go of my hand as he marched me home, my feet struggling to keep up with his long strides. When we reached our house, he took me through the kitchen and proceeded to my parents' bedroom. He yanked me in and threw me onto the bed. As I came down, my head hit the headboard of the bed with a loud *crack!* I immediately burst into tears. Dad said nothing, but continued to give me that dark look. After a moment, he stepped out and closed the door behind him, leaving me there.

This was the moment I knew that there were rules and they were not meant to be broken. This was the day my light started to dim.

My dad was an ambulance attendant. He worked during the day, but it wasn't uncommon for him to be called out in the middle of the night. My mom worked shifts as a nurse and, because of this, I was often left with a babysitter, Mrs. Jenkins.

Mrs. Jenkins was an elderly lady who lived in the apartments on the next block. I didn't know how old she was, but she must have been old because she didn't walk very fast. She had short gray hair that she permed every four weeks, making her resemble an aged poodle. I was always fascinated by her hands. They were always clean, her nails precisely filed. Everything was very precise with Mrs. Jenkins. Her blouse was carefully pressed, she never wore pants, but skirts that ended well below her knee, and she wore sensible shoes with rubber soles, no heels or laces. She was very particular about how to do anything from washing dishes to making tea.

Despite her quirks, I liked her. She treated me well and read me stories. Whenever both my parents were working, she'd come over and take care of me. Like a grandma, sweet and kind but no-nonsense. It was Mrs. Jenkins who called my dad the day I went to Suzy's house, and it was Mrs. Jenkins who comforted me when my dad went back to work. It was Mrs. Jenkins who explained to me that my father was angry because he had to leave work to come and look for me. My dad's anger shocked and hurt me. He had never acted like that before. I couldn't trust my dad anymore. I didn't trust Mrs. Jenkins, either—I felt if she hadn't called my dad I would never have seen that darkness in his eyes. That anger. I decided on that day that I would never make my dad angry again. That was the first of my own personal list of rules.

They say rules were made to be broken. They are wrong.

From that day forward, I did everything in my power to avoid my dad's anger. Before I did anything, I carefully weighed whether or not it would make him angry. Unfortunately, my dad made it difficult to tell what made him happy. A man of few words, he would come home from work, grab a bottle from the cupboard over the fridge, and poor the golden liquid in a glass. He'd take his drink to the living room and turn on the television. I would quietly play on the floor while he watched the news and my mother made supper. I knew better than to talk when he had that empty look in his eyes, staring at the screen and drinking as the announcer went over the day's events. When my mom called us for supper he would grab his glass from the coffee table beside his chair and say, "Let's eat." I would follow him to the kitchen and crawl into my chair without a word.

I began to put all of my efforts into avoiding making my dad angry. I worked hard at being a "good girl." I observed my dad closely, reading his expressions to determine if my behavior was making him happy or angry. When he came through the door each night I would assess his mood; if he appeared happy, I could breathe easy. I learned that if he ran his hand through his short, dark hair he was tired or upset, and that was my cue to be on my best behavior. I worked hard to earn his praise: helping my mom set the table, sweeping the floor, or sitting quietly looking through a book. But I wasn't always successful ... sometimes I slipped up and let that inner joy I tried so desperately to keep hidden, out.

Each spring, the school grounds across the street would flood from the snow melting and a huge puddle of water would form between the sidewalk and the row of trees that bordered the school yard. I was warned that I wasn't to go into the puddle because there could be ice underneath and I could drown—but, again, my curiosity got the better of me.

One afternoon, only a few months after I had created that first rule, I found myself knee-deep in the water. I had put on my purple rubber boots, looked both ways at the crosswalk, and headed to the natural pool. I don't know what it was about the water, but it seemed to draw me like a magnet. I slowly waded in, careful of my parents' warnings about the ice underneath. As the cloudy water swirled around my boots, dangerously close to rising over the top, I took another step. Once I was sure of my footing, I waded back and forth through the murky water, watching the ripples as they moved away from me. I discovered the faster I walked the bigger the ripples, which soon became waves that reached the edges of the puddle.

Just as I was making my way to the middle of the huge puddle, my mom caught me. Her angry shout from the top of our front step had me moving to the edge and quickly making my way across the crosswalk to our house.

"Get to the back door and take off your boots," she directed sharply, and opened the front door to go back inside.

I knew I had broken a rule. With my head down, I slowly trudged to the back door.

She was there to greet me with her arms folded and a frown on her face. "Just wait until your father gets home," she warned, turning back to finish the sinkful of dirty dishes.

I left my boots on the step to dry and stripped off my soggy socks. I went to my room and changed into dry pants and headed for the living room. I spent the afternoon with a ball of nervous anxiety in my stomach. The feeling was like a sickness that was slowly eating away inside of me. Always with me. I dreaded the moment my dad would walk through the door at the end of the day. I silently berated myself for breaking a rule. No amount of apologizing would sway him. He would be furious and I would again see that dark look in his eyes and feel the anger radiating from him.

There was no supper for me that night; after my dad expressed his disappointment in my actions, I was sent to bed for the evening with another harsh reminder that made it difficult to sit down the next day.

I vowed, as I laid with my head on my pillow and tears silently rolled down my cheeks, that I would never break the rules again. That I would always be on my best behavior and make my father proud. The problem was that I never knew if he was proud, but I did know if he was angry.

By the time I turned five, the need to please my parents had become an obsession. I did what I needed to do to prevent my dad's anger, but I was also looking for his love and attention. It seemed that as long as I did what I was told, he would be happy. But not listening to my father would come with a price.

We were at my Uncle Frank's cabin on Lost Lake the summer before I turned five. I loved the lake. The cabin was rustic, built out of plywood with no insulation. The only source of heat was an old stove in the kitchen. There was no bathroom, just an outhouse up a narrow trail behind the cabin that smelled of—well, you know what it smelled of—and spider webs that caught you right in the face when you opened the door.

Despite the lack of modern conveniences, I loved it there. I would spend hours on the hill behind the cabin, picking wildflowers and chasing butterflies in the tall prairie grass. Our visits to the cabin usually involved my aunts, uncles, and cousins. We would pack coolers, inner tubes, and mattresses and head down the gravel road to the nearby beach. Afternoons were spent swimming in the brown water, building sandcastles, jumping off the dock that extended into the water. When the sun started to dip in the sky, we would climb the path to the road, our sandals slipping on the long grass. On our arrival back at the cabin, my dad would fill the barbeque with charcoal briquettes and squirt a generous amount of lighter fuel on them so when he lit them there would be a burst of fire high in the air. My mom and aunts would whip up huge bowls of potato and macaroni salad, while my dad would barbeque burgers and hot dogs. The delicious smells filled the air around the cabin with smoke.

It was tradition that after supper a huge bonfire was built in the yard to roast marshmallows over. On this particular night, the fire was roaring and all the kids were sitting around the fire. We had scavenged in the trees around the cabin for sticks and my cousin, Lee, who was fifteen, used his jackknife to give them each a pointed end for our marshmallows. We each grabbed marshmallows from the bag and pushed them onto the ends of our roasting sticks. The fire had burned down to embers and Lee, who was sitting on my left, had just put a huge log on the fire. He sat in a lounger beside me while the rest of us stood around the fire. I loaded my stick with four marshmallows and stuck it out over the embers closest to me, trying not to get them too close to the flames. I liked my marshmallows golden brown, which meant slowly turning them so they didn't catch on fire. After what seemed like forever, I inspected my marshmallows and saw they were nearly browned to perfection—one more turn and they would be ready to eat.

That was when I heard my dad yell.

"Hannah! You've got too many marshmallows on your stick. They're going to end up in the fire! I told you two marshmallows at a time. Pay attention!"

As I turned to look at him, my foot caught in the leg of Lee's lounger. Feeling myself fall, I stretched my arms out to catch myself. My elbows landed on the huge log Lee had just put on the fire—but from the searing pain in my legs, I knew I had not completely escaped the embers.

The next thing I remembered was Lee carrying me to the cabin, towels laid on my legs, the sounds and movement of a car while my mom held me in her lap, my screams filling the car …

Later, as I lay on the hospital bed, my legs bandaged and sore, my father's words came back to me. He was right—I needed to pay attention. But not to the marshmallows. I needed to pay attention to the rules. If I had listened to my father, I wouldn't be in the hospital with third degree burns to my legs. Ignoring the rules would leave scars that lasted a lifetime.

My first day of school I wore a peach-colored dress with a Peter Pan collar, short cap sleeves and full ruffled skirt. I felt so pretty in that dress. My mother had cut my hair—straight bangs and straight on the sides. I was excited to start school, couldn't wait to meet new kids. Being the only child on my block, I anticipated a wealth of friends and great adventures.

My mom walked me to school that first day. We entered through one of the large double doors and traveled down what seemed to be a never ending hallway. My mom pulled me to a doorway with her hand on my shoulder and I walked into the room in front of her. Low tables and chairs, shelves with books on them, blue mats in the far corner. Pictures covered the walls. Bears of different colors with strange symbols underneath danced across the top of the black-boards. There were a number of other children already in the classroom, sitting at the tables.

I left my mother and headed toward the books. As I went to reach for one, a voice behind me directed, "We will read books later. Right now let's find your seat. What's your name?"

I turned to see a woman older than my mother—in fact, she reminded me of Mrs. Jenkins: gray hair, black-rimmed glasses, a printed blouse, dark brown skirt and the same sensible shoes. She was bent over with her hands on her knees.

I looked at my mom, who raised her eyebrows in what I thought was a silent message to tell this woman who I was. I looked back at her and replied, "Hannah."

"Hello, Hannah. Welcome to kindergarten. I'm Mrs. Randall and I'm your teacher," she said. "Let's find your seat."

She led me to one of the round tables nearest the blackboard and showed me my name tag taped on the table. She pulled out my seat and I sat down. My mom gave me a quick kiss on the cheek and left for work.

To my left, a blond-haired, blue-eyed boy sat staring at me.

"What's wrong with your legs?" he asked.

"Nothing," I answered.

"Yes, there is. Look at them. They look funny." He pointed to my shins where the skin was pink and shiny from the marshmallow fire.

I looked at the scarred area—he was right, they did look funny. Suddenly my cheeks were burning. I pulled my dress over my legs to cover them.

"I burned them," I told him.

"Well, they look ugly," he noted and turned to the girl on his right. I looked down at my hands on the table as I felt tears filling my eyes. He was right—they were ugly. I looked at the other girls in my class with their pretty dresses and no scars on their legs. I wished I looked like they did.

That was Brady. I learned his name ten minutes later when Mrs. Randall made us stand up and introduce ourselves. When it was my turn I quickly stood up and said, almost in a whisper, "Hannah," and sat down again.

"Can you say that a little louder please?" Mrs. Randall asked with a smile. "I don't think everyone heard you."

"HANNAH!" I yelled out, and again felt my face flush a bright red. The smile fell from Mrs. Randall's face.

"She has ugly legs," Brady interjected, as if the whole class needed to know this about me.

"Brady, that's not very nice," Mrs. Randall told him, but Brady didn't look sorry. He looked at me and gave a smirk.

At that moment I wished I could disappear into the floor.

By that time Mrs. Randall had moved on to the next person and I never heard another name.

At recess I made my way over to the swings and as I reached for the last available one, a hand reached out and grabbed the chain links before I could. Brady turned himself in the swing and looked at me.

"Girls with ugly legs don't get to swing," he informed me.

Rather than sock him in the nose, which was what I wanted to do, I made my way over to the monkey bars. I crawled up the rungs and sat on the top one, alone. No one asked me to play. No one talked to me. Why would they? Who wanted to be friends with the girl with ugly legs? I realized that day that I would need to become as invisible at school as I was at home. With one sentence Brady had sealed my fate as one who was different and, by doing so, determined the course of my time in grade school. Right there on that top rung, I decided on the rule I needed for school: don't give anyone the chance to hurt you. Put up walls around you and let those walls protect you.

I never told my mom what happened that first day of school. I came home after and, while I had a snack at the kitchen table and she made supper, she asked me how my day went.

"Fine," I replied around a mouthful of cookie.

"Just fine?" she asked as she stirred the ground beef in the frying pan. Supper tonight was going to be my favorite, to celebrate my first day of school: spaghetti and meat sauce. I didn't tell her that I wasn't up for spaghetti—in fact, the cookies were already sitting like a lead weight in my stomach.

"What did you do?" she prodded.

Hoping she'd leave me in peace, I gave her: "Not much. Read books. Painted."

She wasn't satisfied. "Who's in your class?"

"I don't remember."

"Well, who did you play with?"

I knew she wasn't going to stop until I gave her something more. "Kathleen," I told her.

Kathleen lived two blocks from me and I'd had a couple of play dates with her over the summer, playing with Barbie dolls and

15

skipping in her driveway. Our mothers knew each other because they were both nurses at the hospital.

But Kathleen wasn't in my class and I hadn't seen her on the playground that day.

I had no problem telling my mother this lie. If I'd told her what had really happened at school, I was afraid of what would happen. Would Mrs. Randall hate me? Would I get in trouble? No, better to tell my mom what she wanted to hear rather than the truth. I finished my cookies and put my empty glass of milk on the counter before heading to the living room to watch television. By getting out of my mom's sight I hoped she'd quit asking me questions and I wouldn't have to lie to her again.

Later, I wished I'd told my mom what happened that first day of school. Brady reminded me daily of my "ugly legs" and had started calling me "Scar-legs." I said and did nothing in response to his taunting. I just took his hurtful words inside. Over time I refused my mom's suggestions to wear dresses to school for special occasions, preferring to wear pants that covered up the scars that my classmates found so revolting. This got trickier near the end of the school year when the sun would beat down during recess and lunch hour—but I refused to change my style, even when my mom would look at me and wonder out loud about my sudden revulsion for cool shorts and dresses.

That year became a lesson on how to keep your classmates from noticing you. I never participated in activities without being asked to first. I spent a lot of time alone.

I had become invisible.

CHAPTER THREE

My first impression was correct. Chip was trouble.

He was also persistent, irritating, and, on the odd occasion, funny. The more I ignored him the harder he tried to insert himself into my life.

On his second day of school I discovered that his locker was right next to mine—what an unlucky coincidence. He wore another *Star Wars*–themed shirt, this one with a picture of Yoda and the caption "My finger you will pull." I rolled my eyes. He grinned widely and asked, "Do you like it?"

I slammed my locker shut in answer and walked away.

He followed me down the hallway.

"So Hannah. Tell me a little about yourself. I mean, if we're going to be friends, we should get to know each other."

Still ignoring him, I kept walking toward Mr. Lucas's science class. When he realized I wasn't going to offer any information about myself, Chip proceeded to give me a crash course in everything Chip Cavanagh.

Apparently, the reason he didn't like to be called "Toby" was because he had been named after his dad, who left his mom and him last summer. His mom gave him the name "Chip" because, since his dad left, he'd "had a huge chip on his shoulder." He told me this as a joke, but all it did was remind me of my own dad, so I wasn't laughing. He didn't elaborate any more, other than to tell me he and his mom, Shelley, moved here after the divorce to be closer to his grandparents. After his dad left, his mom struggled with depression, so his grandparents, thinking that a change would help, moved them to Acadia.

When he stopped talking momentarily—probably to sneak in a breath—I asked: "What's with the T-shirts?"

"What do you mean?" he asked, frowning down at his Yoda shirt.

"You have a thing about *Star Wars* or something?"

"Well, yeah. They're the greatest movies of all time!"

I didn't argue with him. I thought *Star Wars* was pretty cool myself, but I didn't offer up that little tidbit of information. I was still harboring the small hope that he'd get tired of trying to carry on a one-sided conversation with me and leave me alone.

But I underestimated Chip. He was like a yappy Chihuahua when it came to trying to get me to talk to him. Before school, at lunch, after school—every time I turned around, he was there telling me a joke or explaining the movie-making genius of George Lucas. I did my best to dodge him, but the proximity of his locker and the seating arrangements in class made it impossible. More often than not I spent most of the time with my head in my writing notebook, pretending to write. I couldn't actually write anything, though, because there was no way I was giving him the chance to see what I wrote. My writing notebook was my safe place, the only place where I could be myself—no one laid eyes on those pages but me.

In Chip's defense, he had no idea about my invisibility or my rules. I considered telling him, but then immediately dismissed the thought. Just telling him would be breaking my own rules. But every chance he got he'd try to talk to me or get me to do something outrageous. And I just couldn't hide in my notebook forever. After a week of not being able to shake him, I finally broke when he tried to convince me that Darth Vader wasn't the villain but the *hero* of the films.

We were having lunch on the front lawn of the school. Chip had made it a habit to sit with me at lunch, even though I ignored him for the whole forty minutes. Today I tried hiding behind a tree, but bloodhound that he was, he found me. And he finally wore me down.

"That's ridiculous!" I snapped at him. As soon as the words were out of my mouth I regretted them, because the smile that lit up his face was the biggest he'd given me yet (and that's saying something). I had finally admitted that he existed. He'd won.

I huffed out an aggravated breath, ignoring his reaction. "You've got it all wrong. Darth Vader is the antagonist, or the antihero. Miss Thomas taught us the difference when we read *The Outsiders*."

But Chip wouldn't be deterred, and he wouldn't wipe that huge grin off his face. "Darth Vader is only looking out for his son, like any good dad would do. Just because he's aligned with the forces of darkness doesn't mean that he's a bad father," he argued, taking a bite of his sandwich and grinning through the pastrami.

"He spends three movies trying to destroy the Empire and get Luke to join in his evil plot. Those aren't the actions of a hero, Chip. And," I held up my finger for emphasis, "he dies at the end. The hero never dies!" I took a bite of my own sandwich and gave him the same self-satisfied smile he gave me.

Chip finished chewing, swallowed, and took a drink of water. I had no doubt he was just stalling, thinking about how he was going to prove my point wrong.

"Yes, but he doesn't die until the end—the hero's ultimate sacrifice!" He raised his eyebrows and took another bite.

"He should have died! He nearly destroyed the universe, or the good part of it, anyway."

"Nah, he was just misunderstood. Really, the whole plot was his attempt to be reunited with his son. A noble cause." Chip nodded his head, almost as if he were impersonating the Yoda on his shirt.

I shook my head. There was no convincing him, even if his theory was totally illogical. I took another bite of my sandwich.

When I didn't offer up a rebuttal, Chip asked: "You agree that I'm right, then?"

"No, I'm just tired of trying to convince you that you're wrong." And I resigned myself to letting him think he'd won.

Chip couldn't wipe that satisfied smile off his face for the remainder of the lunch hour. I knew he thought he'd won a small victory, and I mentally kicked myself for letting down my guard. I'd opened the door a tiny crack, and I knew that Chip was going to shove his size-eight foot in and force his way into my life.

There was no way Darth Vader was the hero!

* * *

My fears were confirmed the next day in Mrs. Barkowski's math class.

The class was silent as we wrote the unit test on multiplying decimals. Mrs. Barkowski finally sat down at her desk after walking up and down the aisles for the first twenty minutes, answering questions or keeping an eye out for anyone who may have their calculator stashed in their desk. I was glad she'd sat down, as I found it hard to concentrate when she walked around, her heels click-clacking on the floor. I settled in to finish my test when a tapping sound reached my ear. This went on for a few minutes—tap, tap, tap—but I tried my best to block it out, mostly because I realized it was coming from right behind me. Only minutes later, however, I glanced up to find everyone staring at the person behind me, including Mrs. Barkowski.

"CHIP!" her shrill voice pierced the silence of the classroom.

"Huh?" he said. He obviously wasn't aware that he now had everyone's attention.

"It's *pardon*. Not 'huh.' Please quit tapping your pencil on your desk so your classmates can finish their tests in peace." Her voice rose in volume with every word.

"Oh, sorry," he said. I could actually hear the smile in his voice.

Chip didn't fear Mrs. Barkowski's anger. In fact, I think he enjoyed getting her riled up. Mrs. Barkowski must have glared at him for a good minute before going back to marking papers. I never could have handled that glare, but Chip just took it all in stride. I heard his pencil scratching over his paper—scratch, scratch, scratch. He was doodling while I struggled to finish multiplying decimals. The fact that Chip could finish his assignment in ten minutes was beyond irritating. I looked around to see that the rest of the class was working away—all except for Brady, who stared at the bulletin board to his right. He'd only answered one question on the page, his pencil lying forgotten on his desk. Brady spent a lot of time staring at the bulletin board, so this wasn't anything new.

Five minutes passed, and, not surprisingly, I felt a sharp tap on my shoulder and Chip whispered something in my ear. I fanned my hand over my ear, like I was trying to shoosh away an irritating fly, and in the process I whacked Chip in the face.

This did nothing to deter him. He kept pestering me. I felt the anxiety build in my stomach. At any moment, Mrs. Barkowski would hear him. The last thing I wanted was to have her anger directed at me.

"Psst, Hannah," I heard from behind me.

I ignored him. My go-to strategy so far. I needed to find another one, because this one rarely worked. I focused on my textbook and wrote down the next question.

"Hannah!" Chip hissed, louder.

I sighed internally. Ignoring Chip wouldn't work. Rather than not talk to me, he would just get louder, and the chances of getting caught would only increase.

"What?" I whispered back.

"There's basketball in the gym today at noon. We should go."

I almost snorted in surprise. What Chip didn't know, and what I had no intention of ever explaining, was that I didn't do sports—of any kind. Especially group sports. The last time I did was last year, when I tried out for the volleyball team. I didn't really have an athletic bone in my body, but my dad encouraged me to try out. Okay, that's a lie. He told me I needed to do some type of activity after school rather than sitting at home with my head stuck in that "stupid notebook." Rather than cause him to get angry, I decided it would be easier to just try out for volleyball—if I was lucky, I wouldn't make the team. Having zero athletic ability and being pretty much paralyzed in situations that involve large groups of people—a recipe for disaster.

Four practices were scheduled before the first game. For the first practice, Coach Sanders had us partner up and do bumping and setting drills to determine our level of skill. My partner was Alyssa, who, like me, had just about zero athletic abilities. We managed to get through the drills with minimal ball chasing and moved on to serving. Trudy, Jill, and Stephanie all stood along the back line, gave their balls a couple bounces, threw them up, and delivered textbook serves over the net. When it was our turn, Alyssa and I both leaned in with the ball in front of us and watched our under-hand serves plough into the net. This went on for about ten minutes, during which time, I got exactly two over the net and Alyssa got three. Keeping track on his clipboard, Coach Sanders praised Trudy and Jill on their serves, while telling Alyssa and I to "keep practic-ing girls, you'll get it."

The last half hour of practice was to be a scrimmage. Coach di-vided us into teams of eight and the first six players took the court. He stood off the court with his running shoe propped on one of the benches, whistle at the ready. Jill served for the other team and the ball came right for Alyssa and me in the back row. We both watched the ball come toward us, arms out, ready to bump it back, when it landed between us. We both stared at the spot where the ball had landed and then at each other.

Coach Sanders clapped his hands and called out, "Hannah! Alyssa! You've got to move to the ball. Make sure you call it, so you know who's going to get it."

We both nodded our heads in his direction and readied ourselves for the next serve. Jill served another one into the same spot. This time we both went for the ball and it bounced off one of my arms and one of Alyssa's and flew wildly toward the wall.

"Good job, girls. You're both moving your feet to get the ball—now call it first," Coach reminded us, rubbing a hand over his bald head.

Jill's next serve was to Trudy, who was also in the back row. She called "Got it!" and moved under the ball, hitting it to Stephanie in the first row, who tipped it over the net.

"Great bump, Jill!" Coach Sanders gave her two thumbs up.

Stephanie bounced the ball at the back line and served a bullet over the net. Jill returned it and again it was coming right for me. I stuck my arms out to bump it. Rather than landing on my forearms, it hit above my elbows and immediately bounced up and hit me in the face.

At that moment all I wanted was for the floor to open up and swallow me. A couple of the girls covered their smiles with their hands. Trudy and Jill were more obvious. They laughed out loud and I flushed with embarrassment. Coach Sanders waved his arm for me to come to the bench, while pushing Becky onto the court to take my place. I made my way to the bench, my eyes on the floor. My face still stung from the hard slap of the volleyball. I sat down beside Jessica.

"You all right?" she asked.

"Yeah, I'm fine," I replied. But I wasn't fine. What was I thinking? Everyone on the team knew I wasn't any good at volleyball. I was kidding myself if I thought I was going to make the team. I stared at the red line that outlined the court. I decided then and there I wouldn't be back.

* * *

"Chip, I don't do noon basketball. Or any basketball for that matter," I told him.

I couldn't see his expression behind me, but I could just imagine that quizzical look, with the cocked eyebrow. "Why not?"

"Because I'm not good at it, and I'm not going to embarrass myself in front of half of the student body." The student body would most definitely include Jill, Trudy, and Stephanie, who were not only volleyball stars, but basketball stars too.

"Why would you be embarrassed? It's just for fun," Chip countered.

"Not for me," I replied and continued to finish my math assignment.

After that, Chip was uncharacteristically quiet.

* * *

I sat alone eating my lunch on the school's front lawn. Once I'd finished my sandwich and yogurt, I occupied myself by pulling grass out of the lawn. A jean-clad, *Star Wars* T-shirted body landed beside me. I didn't acknowledge Chip's presence, just kept plucking at the grass.

"What're you doing?" he asked.

"Nothing."

"So let's hit the gym and see what's happening!"

"Chip, I told you—there is no way that I'm going to play basketball. Give it a rest."

"We'll just go watch. Coach Sanders lets people sit around the gym and cheer if they aren't playing. It's better than sitting out here and killing the lawn," he said, grinning.

"I'm good with killing the lawn."

"C'mon, Hannah. Please! We'll just watch."

"Just watch?" I asked skeptically, looking him in the eye for the first time. He nodded his head enthusiastically and jumped up. He grabbed my hand to pull me up as I brushed the evidence of the lawn's death from my jeans. Chip turned and headed to the front entrance, but I took my time following, scuffing my sneakers along the sidewalk as I went. Anything to slow down our arrival at the gym. Chip waited at the door, holding it open for me, and I passed by him into the hallway. I could hear yelling coming through the doors of the gym on my right, and the sound made my stomach ache. I grabbed the door and stuck my head in. Chip came up behind me and put his hand on my back, subtlety urging me forward. I dug my heels in and then felt a good shove from behind, propelling me forward. My arms windmilled as I tried to keep my balance, but thankfully nobody seemed to have witnessed my near faceplant into the floor.

"Chip!" I hissed, wheeling around, and planted both hands on his chest and shoved him back.

"What?" he returned with a feigned look of innocence. "Come on, let's sit over here."

We made our way to the benches on the righthand side, passing by other onlookers who were trying to pass the noon hour with some entertainment. I sat down on the bench and watched the co-ed teams run up and down the court.

"I'll be right back," Chip informed me.

"Where are you going?" I asked.

"I have something I have to do."

"Whatever." Now he'd gotten me in here to watch, and he abandons me the minute we get here? Typical Chip.

The game was a close one and the red shirts had a six point lead. Both Stephanie and Jill were running up and down the court, looking fresh as daisies. They handed out high fives every time they scored a point.

Chip arrived back and we sat in silence for the next five minutes as the teams battled up and down the court. After Jill took a foul shot, Coach Sanders blew his whistle. Taking his glasses from the top of his head and studying his clipboard, he shouted: "Okay, that's ten minutes, let's change out. Up for the red team: Jessica, Brady, Cole, Chip, and Hannah. Hustle and get on the court!"

Hannah? Was I hearing things correctly? I turned to Chip, who had already gotten up off the bench. I grabbed his arm and turned him toward me.

"Why are they calling our names? You said we would come in and watch. Watch, Chip. Not play!"

"It'll be fun, Hannah! Come on, live a little," he begged.

"No, it will not be fun, it will be torture," I hissed, crossing my arms defensively.

"Well, it's too late now because I wrote your name down and Coach Sanders called you. Let's go!"

At that moment Coach Sanders yelled, "Chip! Hannah! Let's get going, we only have time for one more group to play."

"No," I refused. "I'm not playing."

"Hannah, now," Coach ordered.

I shot Chip the evilest glare I could come up with and made my way to Coach Sanders to get my red shirt. I snatched it out of his hands and pulled it over my head.

"I'm going to stand beside the key and not move," I sulked to Chip, and headed over to the right side of the court. Brady moved to the center for the jump ball and everyone else formed a circle. I knew I looked like an idiot, but there was no way I was going to touch that ball for the next ten minutes and prove how inept I was. Brady won the jump and took the ball down the court for a layup, giving our team an eight point lead. Trudy got the ball for the blue team and dribbled down the court—straight toward me as I hung out under our basket.

She wasn't looking down as she dribbled, but straight at me. I knew enough about basketball to know I should put my hands up and stop her from getting to the net, but I was still angry about Chip tricking me into playing. I kept my hands locked at my sides. I figured if Trudy saw I wouldn't try to stop her, she'd dribble around me. The closer she got, however, I realized that Trudy wasn't going to go around me, but through me. At the last moment, I planted my feet and threw my arms out to the side. Trudy's elbow caught me right in the solar plexus, my feet left the floor, my body sailed backward, and my back slammed against the floor, followed by my head. I couldn't catch my breath. I lay paralyzed, not being able to breathe as my red-shirted teammates gathered around me. I finally took a heaving breath and let it out. The next one was easier and the stars that had been dancing in front of my eyes slowly disappeared. I blinked and saw Chip leaning over me with his hands on his knees, looking at me with concern. Voices started to come to me.

"Is she okay?"

"Did you see her fly through the air?"

"That's gotta hurt!"

Coach Sanders pushed his way through the group and stared down at me. "You all right, Hannah?"

Not sure if I was all right or not, I didn't respond.

"Hannah, how many fingers am I holding up?"

Coach held up four fingers and I wheezed out, "Four."

"Good, good," he replied. "She's going to be okay, everyone. Move back and give her some room."

The group of gawkers slowly moved back and Coach Sanders put an arm under my back to help me sit up. The room seemed to spin for a moment and then cleared. Coach patted me on the back.

"Do you think you can get up, Hannah?"

I nodded my head and bent my knee, forcing myself to stand. I wobbled for a minute. Coach put his hand out to steady me.

"I'm fine," I reassured him.

"Go have a seat on the bench until you feel better," he said.

I made my way to the bench and sat down. That was when I noticed every set of eyes in the gym looking at me. I dropped my gaze to the floor and hoped that I felt good enough to get out of here as soon as possible, to become invisible again.

"Trudy," I heard Coach Sanders call. "That kind of rough play is not acceptable during recreational basketball. I think you need to take a week off and think about what happened here."

I looked up to see Trudy's reaction. Trudy opened her mouth to argue with Coach, but when she saw the look on his face, she quickly snapped it shut, turning on her heel and heading to the girl's locker room. She banged the door open with her hand, and just before the door closed behind her she shot me a killing glare over her shoulder.

Chip sat down beside me on the bench and put his elbows on his knees.

"I'm sorry, Hannah," he apologized. "I didn't think anything like this would happen.

I couldn't even look at Chip. I got up and walked out the gym door.

CHAPTER FOUR

A week later, I still hadn't talked to Chip since the fiasco in the gym. Trudy shot daggers at me every chance she got. When I walked down the hallway, students would turn and look at me while whispering to their friends. This was usually followed by some smart comment like "How's your head, Hannah? I hear they repaired the floor where you cracked it."

My anger toward Chip escalated with every jab. I worked hard to be invisible. I never did anything to draw attention to myself, and I liked it that way. It was *the* rule, but Chip had blown all of my hard work out of the water. I didn't think I could forgive him. I regretted letting him in, because what happened was exactly what I was afraid of and worked so hard to prevent. He didn't understand that, while he didn't care what other people thought, I most definitely did—and now I was the center of attention. I was embarrassed, I was humiliated, and I was hurt. The walls I worked so hard to protect myself with were getting battered every day. More than ever, I wished that I was invisible once again.

Chip was relentless in his attempts to get me to talk to him again. It started the day after the game. He tried to talk to me on four different occasions during the day, but I refused to even look at him—I just stared past him and kept right on walking, pretending that *he* was the invisible one. The next day it was notes. Notes on my desk, shoved into my locker, and in my backpack. They read, "Hannah, I'm sorry," and, "Hannah, please talk to me." I didn't know how he managed it, but I remained steadfast in my resolve not to talk to him. On Friday, he put a bunch of flowers on my desk. I had a sneaking suspicion they came from Mrs. Parker's flowerbed across from the school. When I saw them on the lab bench we shared for science, I stopped in my tracks. I looked at Chip, who had a hopeful look on his face, and slammed my books down. I picked up the flowers and threw them in the garbage without a second look. I felt bad when I saw the look of defeat on Chip's face, his shoulders slumped forward, but I brushed the feeling off and took my seat, not looking in his direction for the rest of the period. It seemed that Chip was just as determined as I was—yesterday Mrs. Barkowski threatened to send him to detention if he didn't quit whispering in my ear during math.

Chip's attempts to get back into my good graces hadn't gone unnoticed by my classmates either. Now, instead of comments about my basketball mishap, I could hear them snickering every time they saw me or Chip. It seemed that Chip and I were both becoming the brunt of everyone's jokes, and while it didn't make me feel any better, I did feel less alone. I took some satisfaction in his discomfort. Why should I be the only one suffering at the hands—or should I say *mouths*—of our classmates?

I'd just rounded the corner to go to the girl's washroom between classes when I ran into Chip, literally. My forehead connected with his chin and we both jumped apart, me rubbing my head, him his chin.

"Sorry," I mumbled. I tried to step around him to the bathroom door. Chip stuck his hand out and stopped me. I looked at his hand on my arm and then up at his face. There was a bright red mark on his chin where we collided, but his eyes held regret, not pain.

"It's okay, Hannah, I deserve it," he said. "I probably deserve a whole lot worse than a smack on the chin for embarrassing you and getting you hurt. I thought, wrongly, that if you just tried basketball that you would see how much fun it is. Instead, Trudy tackles you like a linebacker and the rest of the school makes fun of you for it. I never intended for any of this to happen."

"Don't worry about it," I mumbled, staring at the tops of my shoes.

"I need to know that you forgive me. That we're okay," he said. He bent at the waist so he could look me in the eye, so I shifted my gaze over his shoulder at the row of lockers that lined the hallway.

"We're fine," I mumbled, a bit stronger.

"Look at me, Hannah," he said, and my eyes slowly came back to his.

He looked at me sheepishly from under the lock of hair that fell over his eye. The look of regret on his face was what did me in. I had tried to deny it, but my anger had been fading with each outrageous gesture he used to try and win me over, and that look of regret finally made me cave.

"I forgive you, Chip," I said resignedly.

Immediately, his eyes lit up and he gave me a broad smile. He caught me off guard, then, pulling me in for a hug. My hands hit his chest, my left on Han Solo's face and my right on Leia's as they took a selfie. *Where does he get these shirts?* I wondered to myself. *Geez.* I pulled my head back to look at Chip. He was still smiling. I gave him a tentative smile back.

"Thanks, Hannah," he said. Now there was relief in his eyes instead of regret.

"You're welcome," I said.

"Well, well, look at this!"

Both Chip and I froze at the same time. He took his hands from my arms and the happy look on his face from seconds ago vanished. I knew from the voice that Trudy stood behind me, and in a rush I knew that our awkward hug was going to be all over the school in a matter of minutes. I slowly turned around to see Trudy leaning against the wall, her arms crossed over her chest and an evil smile on her face. She clearly thought she'd caught us in a compromising situation.

"The two love birds hugging it out in the hallway," she exclaimed in a tone filled with glee. Before either Chip or I could say a word, she turned on her heels and disappeared into Miss Thomas's English class.

I knew my face was beet red from embarrassment—I could feel the heat burning my cheeks—and when I turned around I noticed Chip was staring at where Trudy was standing. He still had that goofy smile on his face. I hit him in the chest with the back of my hand.

"You do realize that she's going to tell everyone she saw us hugging in the hallway?" I asked.

"So?" he countered. When he saw the expression on my face, the smile dropped from his. "Don't sweat it, Hannah! We shouldn't care what they think!"

I opened my mouth to argue with him, but thought better of it, realizing it would just be a losing battle. Besides, it appeared Chip and I were over our tiff, so I resigned myself to being in the spotlight again—but at least this time I'd have Chip with me. Misery loves company.

Chip and I entered English class. Sure enough, Trudy was huddled at the back with Brady, Stephanie, and Jill. She had her back to us, so she didn't see us come in and her voice carried across the classroom.

"… they were hugging right outside the girl's washroom door! I know I surprised them, but they just carried on like I wasn't even there," she lied to her captivated audience. She stopped and all three sets of eyes turned in our direction. When they saw Chip and I standing inside the door of the classroom, all three broke out into similar smirks. I ducked my head and, with my eyes on the floor, made my way to my desk by the windows. I plunked my books on my desk, opened my copy of *Hatchet*, and started reading. Chip sat behind me to another eruption of giggles from the group. I forced myself to keep my eyes on the page of my book.

Miss Thomas entered the room at that moment carrying a stack of papers and a cup of coffee. "Let's find our seats, people," she instructed, sitting on the edge of her desk. "Yesterday I assigned you chapter four for homework. Who's got that done? Put up your hands." She took a stack of papers off the top of the pile on her desk.

I raised my hand along with the majority of the class.

"Good. Mr. Robinson, what's your excuse?" she asked. Brady shifted uncomfortably in his seat, his long legs banging on the bottom of his desk.

"No excuse, ma'am," he mumbled into his book, refusing to meet her eyes. Unlike Mrs. Barkowski, Miss Thomas didn't let Brady slack off in class.

"Well, you can meet me in the detention room at lunch," she informed him.

Brady groaned loudly and said something under his breath that sounded a lot like "old bag."

"What was that, Brady?" Miss Thomas inquired, giving him a pointed look.

"Nothing," he replied sullenly.

"That's what I thought. Now, Trudy will hand out the questions for chapter four. Remember to answer each question in complete sentences, please." Miss Thomas handed the pages to Trudy and sat at her desk.

Trudy made her way slowly up and down the aisles giving flirty smiles to some of the boys and flicking the papers on to the desks of those she deemed beneath her. Chip and I were the last ones to get ours. When Trudy finally held her hand out to give them to us she pursed her lips and made kissing sounds. I grabbed the sheets from her hand and scowled at her. She smirked and returned to her seat. I handed Chip's paper to him and settled down to answer my questions.

Ten minutes later and I still hadn't answered a single question. My mind could only focus on what Trudy saw in the hallway. I knew her version of the events would be all over the school by the end of the day. I plotted how I could come down with a deadly disease that would convince my mother that I can't possibly attend school tomorrow. As I went through the most probable options for my demise, a note landed on my desk. Not seeing what direction it came from and thinking Chip threw it on my desk, I opened the paper to find a pair of bright red puckered lip marks on the page. I looked up to see Jill laughing behind her hand and tapping Trudy on the shoulder. She whispered something in her ear and they both laughed quietly.

"Something I can help you with, ladies?" Miss Thomas asked.

"No, ma'am," they replied in unison, like they were twins who finished each other's thoughts. *I thought there was only supposed to be one evil twin,* I thought, smiling to myself.

I took the paper in my hand and crumpled it into a ball before shoving it in the pocket of my hoodie. If that was any indication of what we were in for, I definitely needed to come down with something by tomorrow.

As I walked through the front doors to head home at the end of the day, it seemed like I was running the gauntlet of people making smacking noises with their lips. With my head down, staring at my trusted Chucks, I pushed my way out the door, but not before I heard Brady yell: "Hey Hannah, did Chip kiss your booboo all better?"

Yep, something life-threatening was in order.

CHAPTER FIVE

A pair of red plastic lips sticking out of the vents of my locker greeted me the next morning. Yes, I was back at school—my mother refused to buy my sudden case of malaria this morning. She finally whipped my covers off, after calling me twice and not getting any response.

"Hannah, you're going to be late for school if you don't get out of bed."

"I'm not going to school today," I murmured, covering my head with my pillow and pretending to be half asleep.

"Why not?" she asked, giving me a look of concern, her hands balanced on her hips.

"I think I have malaria," I said.

"Malaria!" she spat out in a shocked voice. And then she started laughing. "Hannah, you can't have malaria."

"Why not?" I grabbed the covers and pulled them back over me. She wrestled them away again.

"First, malaria is transferred from mosquitoes and it's November. Second, those mosquitoes are only found in tropical climates, which, in case you haven't noticed, we do not live in. Now, get your butt out of bed."

I rolled over and faced the wall, ignoring her. I knew she hadn't left the room, and I waited for what I knew was coming.

She didn't disappoint—less than a minute later I heard: "Seriously, Hannah. I don't have time for this!"

"Well, maybe it's not malaria," I attempted. "Maybe it's a really contagious form of the flu and I shouldn't go spreading it around." I gave a half-hearted cough.

"Out! Now!" my mother demanded, turning to storm through the door.

I lay with a sick knot of dread in my stomach. Maybe I really had convinced my body that I was sick, because every time I thought about going to school I felt like throwing up. I looked at the clock on my nightstand: seven forty-five. If I held out a little longer I would be late for my first class.

"Hannah!"

I pulled myself into a sitting position on the edge of the bed, resigned to the fact that I was going to have to get up and head to school. I grabbed my jeans off the floor and a T-shirt out of the drawer, got dressed, and walk into the kitchen to find it empty. Obviously, my mother had left for work. The thought skittered across my mind to not bother going to school at all—but there was no way I'd face my dad's anger if he found out I'd skipped school. School was definitely the lesser of two evils. I reached for a banana on the counter. That would be the only thing my stomach could handle at the moment. Heaving my backpack over my shoulder, I locked the door and set out for school.

My stomach started doing flip-flops as soon as the school came into sight. A mass of students lounged on the front steps waiting for the bell to ring. I slowed down and came to a stop at the bottom of the steps, lingering rather than making my way through the crowd above me. I leaned against the rails and faced the houses across the street. A few students passed me, but I avoided eye contact. Suddenly, my knee went out from under me and I slid to the left, straight into Chip, who had that mischievous smile on his face.

"Morning!" He sounded way too enthusiastic.

"Morning," I replied with no enthusiasm at all.

"Why so glum?"

I gave him a look that said, *"Really?"*

"Oh, I don't know," I said, "just waiting to see what Trudy and her crowd have in store for me today."

"Don't worry about them, Hannah," Chip reassured me. "They can only bother you if you let them. So don't let them."

"Easy for you to say. They aren't making kissing sounds or smacking their lips every time they see you."

"No," Chip replied. "I get comments that are cruder."

"You do?"

"Yeah, and that was before yesterday." He looked up the steps to the group gathered at the landing that includes Trudy and Brady. I followed his gaze and saw them laughing at another student who was making his way into the school.

"They're idiots," I said.

"Yep, and that's what you need to remember when their comments start to get to you."

I paused, considering what Chip said. He was right. I saw them as idiots when they harassed other people, but took it all in when they directed it at me.

"C'mon," he said. "Let's go in before the bell rings."

I followed him up the steps. When we got halfway up, the morning bell rang. The lounging students all jumped up and we entered with the sea of kids.

* * *

Chip's advice from the morning stuck with me all day. I ignored the whispered and not-so-whispered comments. I even felt pretty good about myself—until last period science with Mr. Lucas.

When we entered, Mr. Lucas was standing behind the lab bench at the front. His wiry red hair bounced around his head as he greeted each of us. Today's assignment was an experiment on creating circuits, and Mr. Lucas had us working with our lab partners at stations around the perimeter of the classroom. Chip and I had been assigned to the station near the front. With our textbooks and lab sheets set up in front of us, we tried to follow the directions for creating a parallel circuit. The rest of the class worked quietly, with the odd murmur of voices. Mr. Lucas, his hands stuck in his white lab coat, circulated around the class giving advice and posing questions to the different groups.

During one of the quiet moments in class, a sudden bark of laughter erupted. This wasn't anything unusual for lab work, so I carried on trying to get the wires correctly connected to make our circuit work. It wasn't until I heard "I wish my life was different" that I froze. Chip gave me a curious look. I didn't turn around at the sound of Brady's voice. All the blood drained from my face.

"Are you okay?" Chip asked me.

I didn't answer. I stared at my hands holding the wires—they were shaking.

"Hannah, what's wrong?" Chip asked again. "You look like you're going to faint!"

He was right—I felt like I was going to faint. Light-headed. Dizzy. Petrified of what would happen in the next moment. I hoped that if I didn't show any reaction, nothing would happen—but I was never that lucky.

" 'I wish that I was different' " came from the back of the room again. "Different? Yeah, I would say you don't need to wish for that, Hannah. You've got it nailed," Brady announced to the classroom. His voice reached the farthest corners. I felt my shoulders come up to my ears in humiliation. I still hadn't turned around to acknowledge him. I couldn't. I waited, hoped he'd be discouraged by my lack of reaction. But, like I said, I was never that lucky.

I wish I were someone else was the next line in the poem—*my* poem—and I held my breath, waiting for those most private words to come out of Brady's mouth.

I wasn't disappointed.

And my body unfroze and I whirled around and stormed to the back of the room where Brady stood holding my writing notebook, and I made a grab for the book and missed as Brady raised his hand in the air putting the notebook out of my reach. By now everyone in the class looked at me as I jumped to try and grab the notebook from his hands.

He tilted the book to read the next line. " 'I wish …' " was all he got out before Mr. Lucas walked over and snatched the book from Brady's hand.

Mr. Lucas handed it to me. "That will be enough, Brady," he ordered.

Brady looked at me and laughed. "Sure, Mr. Lucas, no problem." He headed back to his station and his partner, Trudy.

Mr. Lucas put his hand on my shoulder and peered at me with concern. "Do you need a few minutes, Hannah?"

I shook my head and stuffed my notebook in my backpack hanging on the back of my lab chair.

"You might want to put that where prying, nosy eyes can't get at it," he advised.

I nodded my head numbly and walked back to the lab station, where Chip waited with a concerned look on his face.

"You sure you don't want to take a few minutes by yourself?" he asked.

"No, I'm fine," I replied shortly. I grabbed the wires for the circuit.

At the bell, I slung my backpack off my chair and raced for the front doors. Chip yelled for me to wait for him, but I ignored him and raced down the steps of the school, determined to get home as fast as I could.

I walked through the door and headed directly to my room. I slammed the door and dropped my backpack to the floor. Keeping my arms at my sides, I let gravity take me and fell face first on the bed. It didn't take long for the tears to slowly start tracking down my face. I had never been so mortified in my life than the moment I heard my thoughts and feelings come out of Brady's mouth. No one knew about my writing. Not my parents. Not the kids at school. Not my teachers. No one. Keeping my writing to myself was another one of my rules. My writing was for me alone. It was the only place that I let my true self out.

And now Brady had ruined it.

I had no idea how I'd show my face at school the next day. My mom wouldn't fall for another fake attack of sickness, I knew that much—she didn't even fall for the first one. But when I imagined what it would be like to walk down the hallways tomorrow I literally felt like I was going to bring up my lunch. My stomach churned at the thought of someone, anyone, making a comment about what I'd written in my book. It was worse than the kissing noises and re-marks about Chip and I. So, so much worse.

Then—a flash of brilliance! I remembered the thought I'd had this morning as I got ready for school. What if I didn't show up at all?

I suddenly felt confident that it would work. This was the answer. What would I do the next day? I'd worry about that tomorrow. After all, I had all day to plan.

CHAPTER SIX

With my plan firmly in place, I woke up the next morning with dread sitting like a weight in my stomach—but I was determined to go through with it. My mom didn't come and wake me like last time. Today, I was out of bed as usual and dressed for school as she walked out the door for work. My dad stood by the kitchen sink finishing his morning coffee and a piece of toast.

"Hey," I greeted him, confused. He was dressed in his EMT uniform, his hair wet like he'd just gotten out of the shower. "How come you're still here?"

He dusted the crumbs off his hands and took one last sip of coffee before putting the cup and plate in the sink.

"I had a call out last night, so I don't have to be in until eight thirty," he said, grabbing his bomber jacket off the back of a kitchen chair. He shrugged it on and snatched his keys off the counter.

I took an apple from the bowl on the counter and headed for the door. I called over my shoulder, "I'm out of here, Dad. See you tonight."

He gave his typical reply: "Yep, have a good day."

I shouldered my backpack and headed down the path to our front gate. I stopped for a moment, surveying the neighborhood. It looked like it typically did—the McNevins were off to work, and a few kids on their bikes heading to school. No one seemed interested in what I was up to.

I started toward the school. A block down I took a left, rather than continuing on to school, and found myself at the park. I jumped into a swing and pushed off the ground to get it moving. I pumped my legs back and forth, and soon I was flying high into the air. I almost forgot why I was at the park instead of school. As the swing slowly glided to a stop, I got off and sat down at the bench. I slid my writing notebook and pen from my backpack and turned to a fresh page.

I sat and looked at the trees bordering the park. The Brady situation got me thinking. I wondered, like I often do, what life would be like if I were someone else. I bit into the apple and thought what it must be like to not be invisible—to be the real me, not the invisible version of myself. I was no risk taker. I didn't put myself out there, uncaring what people thought or said.

Chip was like that. He was always himself, and if people didn't like it—too bad. I admired that about Chip. It took courage, courage I didn't have. I picked up my pen and started to write. By the time I finished I had a poem that expressed everything I wished I had the courage to do. I didn't have the courage to go to school today and face what was sure to be a mountain of pokes and jabs that would deflate me like a balloon. I wasn't strong enough to face the gleeful jeering of my classmates.

I spent the rest of the morning at the park. As it got closer to noon I started home. My parents didn't come home at lunch, so I planned to spend the afternoon at home safe in the knowledge that my parents didn't get off work until well past the time school was over. I unlocked the front door, anticipating a turkey sandwich and glass of milk for lunch—when I came around the corner to find my dad in the kitchen.

A startled "Oh!" left my lips and I froze in the doorway, too stunned to speak.

My dad turned his head toward me—and I could see that dark look in his eyes again, his mouth in a firm line.

"Hannah! Where have you been?" he asked.

My mouth was dry as I tried to form a convincing excuse or lie to explain why I was home in the middle of a school day. As my mind sorted through a number of possible responses, I noticed my dad was holding a glass of amber liquid in his right hand.

"What are you doing home?" I asked, trying to change the subject.

"The school called your mom this morning when you didn't show up. Apparently she couldn't get away from the hospital, so she called me to come and check on you. I don't have time for your nonsense, Hannah. Would you like to tell me why you aren't in school?" He slammed the glass in his hand on the counter. I jumped at the sound, but the glass didn't break.

"I … uhh …" I stammered, thinking fast. "I forgot my science experiment in my room, and it's due after lunch."

"Go get it and I'll drop you off at school. We'll be discussing this tonight when your mother gets home."

"Okay, I'll just grab my assignment," I answered, and started up the stairs to my room. My mind was swirling with a million thoughts, from how my dad ruined my plans to avoid going to school today, to my worry about how angry he would be. And why was he drinking—at noon? How long had this been going on for?

I rummaged around in my room, in case my dad was listening, and tried to waste some time so it appeared like I was searching for my assignment. After what I considered a reasonable time, I trudged downstairs to the front door. My dad was waiting in the car. The horn honked. I quickly locked the door and got into the car's passenger's side.

As we silently made our way down the street to my school, I worried that he would put two and two together and realize that I skipped class that morning. He didn't say a word, however, during the whole drive, seemingly lost in his own thoughts. He pulled up to the school and I reached for the door handle.

"Thanks for the ride," I said.

He gave me a hard look, but said nothing. I got out of the car. As he pulled away, I looked toward the stairs leading to the school—again swimming in a sea of students—and took a deep breath. I hitched my backpack onto my shoulder and hesitantly walked up the stairs—maybe no one would notice as I made my way into the school.

I stared at my shoes, placing each foot carefully on the steps. My nerves were jangling and I didn't want to draw any attention to myself by tripping up the stairs. My ears were tuned to the sounds around me, listening for any whispers as I passed each group of students hanging around on the steps until the bell rings to begin afternoon classes.

I had just placed my foot on the final step when I heard a voice say: "Hannah? Is that you? I didn't recognize you. Something just seems … *different*."

The laughter that followed was like a bunch of hyenas celebrating a kill. I didn't recognize the voice, which meant Brady's little stunt yesterday had been communicated like an all-points bulletin on a police scanner. Everyone knew.

I ducked my head and grabbed the door as another chorus of laughter sang behind me. Making my way down the hallway to my locker, I was not surprised to see that again something was stuck on my locker.

Wallpapered over every inch of my locker were at least thirty pictures of my yearbook photo—only each one had been altered in some way. In one I had a unibrow, another a different mouth, and still another showed me with a mohawk hairdo. Someone spent a lot of time with Photoshop to come up with all these versions of me. Each one had a speech bubble with words like "I wish I were different" written inside. Tears of humiliation welled up in my eyes. I tilted my head upward, refusing to let them fall. The bell rang, re-placed by the sound of students filling the hallways. I reached up and ripped the pictures from my locker. Before anyone could see them, I stuffed them in my backpack. I turned to go to homeroom and found Brady standing across the hallway staring at me with his trademark smirk on his face.

"Like my gift, Hannah?"

I looked right through him as I walked past—but not before he got in a final shot.

"It's okay to cry, you know. It makes you ... *different.*"

Tightening my grip on my backpack, I walked faster. I refused to give him the satisfaction of seeing me cry over his stupid joke. I practically ran to my desk in Mr. Cooper's room and waited for the rest of the class to file in for attendance. Mr. Cooper, sitting at his desk in his button-down shirt and bowtie, looked at me over the tops of his glasses and said, "Hannah, you need to go down to the office to get your absence excused from this morning."

Crap! I'd forgotten the school policy about excused absences. The fact was, I didn't miss many days of school—and if I did, my mom usually called in. I grabbed my backpack off the floor and headed for the door.

I couldn't believe it. I just faced the wrath of my dad, Brady's bullying, and now I had to explain to Principal Struthers? I'd never been called to the office before—I'd never had to face Principal Struthers.

Could this day get any worse?

I pulled open the door to the office and made my way to the counter. Mrs. Jackson, the school secretary, sat at her desk, her short, dirty blond hair pinned back away from her face. She set aside some forms when she saw me come around to the counter.

"What can I do for you, Hannah?" she asked.

"I ... um, Mr. Cooper told me that I had to come down and get my absence cleared from this morning."

"Let me check today's attendance sheet," she said, scanning a clipboard to her right. "It says here that your mother was called this morning."

"Miss Williams." Principal Struthers stuck his head out of his office door.

"Yessss, sir," I replied.

"Can I see you in my office, please?"

I nodded my head, walking around the counter. He held the door for me as I passed by him to sit in one of the chairs in front of his desk. Once I sat down, the first thing I noticed was how boring his office was. A large desk with nothing on it took up most of the space. Two framed diplomas from universities I'd never heard of hung on the wall. I squinted at one. Mr. Struthers's middle name was Boris? Eww. Mr. Struthers walked around his desk and sat down.

"Hannah, when I called your mother this morning to excuse your absence she told me that she was unaware of any reason for you not to be at school this morning. Would you like to explain that, please?"

For the second time that day, my mind reached for an excuse.

"I got sick on my way to school and went back home," I lied.

"Mmm ..." Mr. Struthers seemed to be pondering the truthfulness of my excuse, tapping one finger on his cheek. When I didn't break his stare, he dropped his hand to his desk. "You know, Miss Williams, that our school has a very strict policy regarding skipping classes. Since your absence was not cleared by your mother and I have no way to verify if you truly were sick on the way to school, I'm going to have to require you make up the time in detention. I'll expect you to spend the next three noon hours in detention. And Miss Wiliams, if you miss any of those noon hours, they will be added to the initial three."

"I understand," I murmured.

"I'll put you on the list for tomorrow. You may return to class."

He took a pen and wrote my name at the bottom of a lengthy list. I was dismissed, so I grabbed my backpack and returned to the counter. Mrs. Jackson gave me a late slip and I headed to French.

Luckily, there were only ten of us in that class. The "in crowd" were too cool for French, so I could breathe a sigh of relief. I took out my notebook and started to conjugate the verbs on the white-board.

I made it through two when my mind began to wander to my latest dilemma. My parents would have some very direct questions for me tonight—and I had no idea what I was going to tell them. Telling the truth would only bring up more questions. Questions I didn't want to answer. I couldn't tell them I skipped school because I was too afraid to face what I was sure would be the whole school laughing at me. I'd already lied to my dad about why I was home—what would I say now? My dad was going to be angry. He despised lying, and my rule about not making my dad mad? This would shatter it. That fluttery feeling settled in my stomach. I needed to come up with some way to get out of this one.

One more period to get through. I both wished it would end and, at the same time, dreaded having to go home and face my parents. I studied the tiles of the hallway down to the science lab, not willing to raise my head and see the amused looks on the faces I passed. Someone jostled my elbow—Chip, smiling at me.

"Hey," he greeted enthusiastically, like he was happy to see me.

"Hey," I answered half-heartedly.

"Missed you this morning. Where were you? Skipping out?" He nudged my elbow again and I gave him an irritated scowl. Some-times his cheerfulness really irked me. That and the fact that he correctly guessed why I wasn't at school.

"Yeah," I said.

"Really?" he said. "Since when do you skip school?"

"Since Brady read my poetry out to the whole class," I muttered. Chip obviously didn't see how embarrassing it was, but then not much bothered Chip. He could care less what other people thought of him, especially people like Brady.

"I know you're upset, Hannah, but to skip school? Why would you let them get to you like that?"

"Because, Chip," and I took a deep breath, "I don't like people knowing my private thoughts!"

"Hannah, he read three lines of a poem. A poem most of us can relate to because we all wish we were different. What's the big deal?"

"The big deal is that I don't want those people in my personal business. That's the big deal," I huffed, and sat on my stool at our bench in the lab.

Chip threw his books on the bench and sat down next to me. "I thought we agreed they were idiots. Who cares what they think?"

"I care," I replied.

"I don't understand, Hannah. Explain to me why you think the opinions of a bunch of idiots should matter to you."

"I can't explain it to you, Chip. I can't even explain it to myself," I answered quietly.

Mr. Lucas stood behind his lab bench and began the day's lesson. Chip searched my face once more before opening his book. Thankfully, he didn't mention it again.

* * *

I sat on my bed after school, my leg bouncing like a basketball. I still hadn't come up with an explanation for my absence at school this morning. My mind was blank. Any story I came up with wouldn't work—Dad had come home to check to see why I wasn't at school.

The front door slammed and my mom called upstairs: "Hannah!"

I considered not responding, but I knew if I didn't it would only make things worse.

"Yeah?" I called back.

"Get down here, please. We need to have a talk."

I felt the sweat start to form on my forehead as I made my way to the bottom of the stairs. My mom was standing in the living room with her hands on her hips. The look on her face–that furrow she gets in her brow—told me that she was not happy, and I prepared myself for what I knew was coming.

"I got a call at work from the school this morning asking me if I had forgotten to clear your absence. At first, I told them there must be some mistake because you were dressed and ready for school when I left for work, but Principal Struthers was adamant that you weren't present in homeroom or first class. Do you want to explain to me why you weren't at school this morning?"

I didn't really, but that obviously wasn't the response she was looking for. Her toe started to tap out a rhythm on the carpet.

"I just … I … um … I got to school and then I realized that I'd forgotten to do my science homework, so I came back home to finish it," I stammered out.

"Why didn't you do it last night?" she demanded.

"I guess I forgot?"

"You forgot, or just didn't do it?" she countered.

"I didn't understand it," I explained. "I left it on my desk, and then I realized when I got to school that it wasn't done and I didn't have it. So I came home and finished it." I hoped my feeble attempt at an excuse would fly, but I wasn't sure.

"Hannah, do you have any idea what it's like to receive a phone call from the principal telling you that your child isn't at school and you have no reason why? It makes me look like I have no clue about what my child is up to."

"No, I don't. I'm sorry."

"Well, next time you have an assignment due and don't understand it, get some help. Skipping school is not an option. Do you have homework tonight?"

"Yes," I told her.

"Get up to your room then and get it done," she said, pointing upstairs.

My dad arrived home a half hour later. I could hear the two of them talking. Pretty soon I got another: "Hannah, get down here!" this time from my dad.

They sat at the kitchen table. I could smell hamburgers cooking on the grill outside the patio doors, but both my parents looked like supper was the furthest thing from their minds.

"Have a seat, Hannah," my dad ordered. "We need to discuss why you weren't at school this morning. Do you know how worried your mom was when she got the call from the school to say you were absent?"

I noticed that he left out that *he* was worried.

"I did explain it to you," I hedged. "I told you that I came home to get my science experiment."

"Yes, you did. But what you failed to mention was that you'd been home all morning." He raised his eyebrows at me. "Why did you omit that important piece of information?"

I could feel myself shrinking under his gaze. My mind searched for a response that would deflate his anger—thoughts bounced around in my head like ping-pong balls, but nothing would come out of my mouth.

"Principal Struthers now believes that your mother and I have absolutely no idea about what our child is up to. Besides that, I had to leave work in order to come home and find out exactly what was going on. I have a job, Hannah, that comes with responsibilities and commitments. I can't just take off at the drop of a hat every time you decide to go on an adventure. You know what? I don't want to hear whatever excuse you have cooked up in your head. You're grounded for two weeks. Home immediately after school and no phone calls from friends. You got it?"

I got it. Detention and now grounded. The grounding wasn't a big deal—I usually came home after school anyway (it was obvious that my parents hadn't noticed), and I didn't get any phone calls from friends other than Chip.

"Set the table for your mother, and when you've finished your supper you can get back up to your room and get your homework done," my dad said.

I remained silent as I ate my burnt hamburger, as did my parents. When supper ended I went to my room and shut the door.

I fumed as I sat there. Like any encounter with my dad, I was in the wrong. Even if I had come up with an excuse—okay, a lie—he would still believe the worst and punish me. The only bright side to all of this was that neither of them had any idea about the real reason I skipped school.

It was going to be a long two weeks.

* * *

Three days later, having just served my final detention, I sat outside, leaning up against the school, when Chip came over and joined me.

"Hey."

"Hey." My usual response to his usual greeting.

"You're finally out of jail," he laughed.

"Yep, finally out," I didn't laugh.

"I've missed you at lunch. It's kinda boring eating by myself. You still grounded, too?" he asks.

"Yes, Chip. I still have another week-and-a-half left on that sentence."

"Bummer," he noted.

I pulled my backpack toward me to get my lunch. Chip reached over and made to grab for my writing notebook.

"What are you doing," I growled.

"I want to see your writing," he explained. "After all, this is what got you into this mess in the first place."

"No one looks in there but me," I informed him, and shoved it aside so he couldn't get his hands on it.

"Hannah, I'm your friend. Why won't you show me some of your writing? I'm sure it's good. Let me read it. Pleeease," he begged.

"Not gonna happen," I declared and took a bite of my sandwich. Showing Chip my writing violated Rule #2: never be vulnerable. And that meant—NEVER!

I learned my lesson about vulnerability a long time ago. Since then I hadn't broken it. Chip thought I was just being stubborn, but that's where he was wrong. I'd learned that when I let people see who I really am, more often than not I ended up getting hurt.

The first and last time I'd been intentionally vulnerable around my peers was Grade 1. My best friend at the time was Katie. Katie and I shared the same haircut, bangs in front and the rest one length that came to our chins. Her hair was a dark blond while mine was whiter. I didn't know Katie before school, she didn't live in my neighborhood. On the first day of school, we were both lining up to go down the slide. I usually stood off to the side to wait for everyone else to go, but Katie motioned for me to go in front of her. Every day after that we spent recesses together and found that we had a lot in common. We shared a love of Barbie dolls, combing their hair and dressing them up. We spent hours playing together.

One day in October, Trudy (yes, she was around even then) was busy putting envelopes on everyone's desk before the second bell rang in the morning. As we filed into the classroom and hung our coats on the hooks at the back of the room, I saw that every girl's desk but mine had a white envelope sitting on it. Trudy was explaining to Stephanie (yes, her too) about the plans for her birthday party. I saw Katie pick up the envelope from her desk and open it. She smiled and came over to me.

"Trudy's having a birthday party!" Katie's eyes were lit up with excitement. "And we need to wear costumes! I'm going to wear the hippie outfit I wore last year for Halloween. I've got a wig with long hair, bell bottom jeans, and a leather headband. What are you going to wear?" she asked breathlessly.

"I didn't get invited," I replied dully, feeling a large lump clog my throat.

"What? How come?" Katie asked.

"I don't know," I managed to force out. I tried to take a deep breath and force down the feeling that I would burst into tears at any moment.

"Are you sure? Maybe yours got lost or stuck to someone else's?" she suggested. "Every other girl got invited, maybe Trudy doesn't realize that you got missed."

My gaze swung from Trudy back to Katie. I looked at her skeptically.

"I'll go ask her," she offered.

She walked over to where Trudy was talking to Stephanie.

"Oh, hi Katie!" Trudy said cheerily. "Are you excited about my party?"

Katie smiled and nodded. "I can't wait!" She cleared her throat. "I was just wondering about Hannah. She didn't get an invitation."

Trudy looked at me then, and with a fake look of sympathy said, "My mom only let me invite ten people. I asked if I could invite everyone, but my mom wouldn't change her mind." She wore a smile meant to be sincere, but I'd been reading people's moods long enough to know that it wasn't genuine.

I looked away. I couldn't stand looking at the satisfied gleam in Trudy's eyes.

I moved toward my desk and Katie followed me. Her small smile was genuine in its concern and sympathy.

"I'm sorry, Hannah," she said. "I honestly thought it was a mistake, not on purpose."

I nodded my head and gave her a weak smile.

The day after the party, Katie avoided me at recess, instead going off to play with Trudy and Stephanie. I didn't understand why she wasn't interested in playing our usual games together. I got up the courage to ask her at lunch what was the matter.

She wouldn't look at me. I knew I wasn't going to like what she had to say.

"Hannah, I'm sorry," she began, "but I can't play with you anymore. Trudy told me that you have some disease and it makes your legs look funny and I don't want to catch it. I can't be your friend anymore."

I didn't know what to say. I couldn't find the words to tell her that I'd burnt my legs in a fire—wasn't that just as bad as having a disease? So I said nothing and she turned and ran to her new friends, with Trudy at the center.

That was the day that I created Rule #2 and I vowed to never put myself out there like that again. I added another brick to my protective wall.

Katie moved away in the spring and I was relieved to no longer have the constant reminder of how I had let my guard down only to get hurt.

* * *

Chip gave me his puppy-dog eyes and I rolled mine at him. No way was he getting a hold of my writing notebook. There was no telling what would happen, to it or me, in his hands. I continued eating my sandwich, ignoring him as he pressed his hands together like he was praying in an attempt to get me to change my mind. He stuck out his bottom lip and got right in my face.

"No!"

"Pretty please, Hannah," he said, followed by his begging expression.

I refused to reply and just kept eating.

When it became apparent that I wasn't going to change my mind, he gave up and dug into his lunch.

"I'm going to wear you down, Hannah. Just wait and see." He took a huge bite out of his sandwich, smiling confidently at me. I didn't acknowledge his declaration, but kept eating my own sandwich. He didn't know it, but I could be as stubborn as he could.

Reading my writing? Not going to happen.

CHAPTER SEVEN

On Saturday night, I sat in my room listening to music. It was the last night of my grounding and I was going stir crazy from spending all this time alone in my room. My parents hadn't spoken to me about my skipping out since the day it happened. Actually, they hadn't spoken to me much at all. I'd been home every day right after school—not that they'd know, because they're both still at work. I only saw them at dinner, which I spent silently, while my parents discussed their day. After silently helping my mom with the dishes, I confined myself to my bedroom.

I'd started to notice something over the last couple of weeks as I removed myself from talking to my parents—other than the usual greetings, my mother and father didn't really talk to each other either. They exchanged information and general interest in how each other's day went, but other than that, there were long silences at our table.

Things were clearly not right with my dad. He seemed perpetually tired, and he must not have been sleeping well because he had bags under his eyes. My dad's silence was what concerned me the most. He only answered the questions my mother asked him. When not answering her questions, he seemed to drift off somewhere. My mom noticed, too, and tried to bring him back from where ever he was by asking him about the weather or what he thought about something in the news. Her attempts didn't always work.

I started thinking about the day I skipped school and my dad drinking while he waited for me to show up. He never mentioned it again, but he had to know that I saw what he was drinking, even if he refused to acknowledge it. I wondered how long my dad had been coming home at lunch with an excuse of some kind in order to slip something out of the cupboard above the fridge.

Tonight, before supper, he sat with a glass in his hand after work, staring at the television. I'm pretty sure he wasn't listening to the sports report and he hardly even blinked at the announcer. He just raised his glass every few minutes and stared at the screen. While I knew better than to bother him when he was like this, something was … different about his mood. I couldn't put my finger on it, and that worried me. He didn't pay attention to what was going on around him, but I was afraid that any little thing could still set him off.

I turned off the lamp and settled under the covers. I rubbed my cold feet against the sheets in an effort to warm them up. I lay in the dark, and that was when the niggling feelings of worry took hold. My dad and I had never been close. He always had a detached air about him. I knew he loved my mom and me, he just didn't show it very often. Lately, however, he seemed more disconnected than usual. I worried that something might be wrong.

I fell into a troubled sleep, until I woke to the sound of the front door closing. I arched my neck at the digital display on my clock. Two fifteen. Who would be coming or going at this hour? Then my parents' discussion at the dinner table came back to me. My dad had mentioned last night that it was his turn to be on call. That meant that at any time during the night, if the ambulance was called out he'd have to go. I rolled onto my left side. It wasn't strange for my dad to get called out in the middle of the night, but, combined with his strange behavior lately, that ball of worry was back rolling around in my stomach. The last time I remembered looking at my clock, it was three forty. I'd been listening for my dad to come home, hoping it was just a quick transport of a patient from one hospital to the other, which happened quite regularly. This was my last thought as I fell to sleep, without hearing my dad arrive home.

I came downstairs Sunday morning to find my dad sitting at the kitchen table in a pair of old sweats and a ratty T-shirt. His hair was a mess and he was holding a cup of coffee with both hands in front of his mouth. I walked by him, but he didn't seem aware of me as I opened a cupboard and grabbed the cereal from the top shelf. I poured a generous amount into a bowl and splashed milk in until the cereal almost reached the brim. With spoon in hand, I made my way to the table, careful not to spill any of my breakfast on the floor.

When I placed the bowl on the table, my dad jumped as if surprised to see me there. The coffee sloshed over the rim of his cup. We both reached for a napkin from the dispenser in the middle of the table before the trail reached the edge of the table.

"Thanks, Hannah," he said as I handed him the napkin. He sopped up the spilt coffee.

I spooned cereal into my mouth. My dad seemed preoccupied by something, so I ate silently. After a few moments he acknowledged me.

"How are you this morning?"

"Okay," I replied. "Tired. Did I hear you leave last night?" I asked the question even though I knew the answer.

"Got a call," he answered, looking out the patio doors.

"What happened?" Suddenly, I wasn't really sure I wanted to know the answer from the strange way he was acting.

"Accident," was all he said, still staring out the window, his hand wrapped around his mug like he was trying to warm himself up. He didn't add any more, and after a few moments I took another spoonful of cereal.

We sat there. When I finished my breakfast I carried my bowl to the sink. My dad still stared out the window. I left him there.

Something had happened, that much was obvious, but I had no idea how to talk to him about it. I went back to my room and crawled into bed.

CHAPTER EIGHT

Monday morning found Chip hanging around my locker before the nine o'clock bell. He wore faded jeans and a black hoodie, one leg bent at the knee resting against the locker behind him. He pushed off the locker the moment he saw me coming down the hall. He flashed me a grin a mile wide, but I didn't return his smile. I had too much on my mind.

He started talking as soon as I got within hearing range.

"So now that you're free again, I think we should do something after school to celebrate," he proposed.

I looked at him with a complete lack of interest.

"You want to celebrate me not being grounded anymore? And how would you suggest we do that?" I asked as I flicked the tumbler on my combination lock and opened my locker to find my math books.

"I don't know. Ice cream after school, since now you don't have to be home right after," he suggested. "I hear they've got some new flavors down at the Milky Way."

Chip was smart—I had to hand it to him. He knew how hard it was for me to resist ice cream. Had he suggested anything else, I probably would have said no, but I never said no to ice cream. It was practically one of my rules.

"Okay," I replied, shutting the door to my locker. I felt bad when

I saw the hopeful look on his face, so I gave him a small smile.

"Awesome!" he exclaimed and raised his hand to give me a high five. It took me a second to understand what he was doing and I missed his hand entirely—but I was successful on my second attempt. I mentally shook my head at my lack of coordination.

After school, Chip was waiting for me on the steps, chatting with a couple of other boys who were waiting as well. When I walked out the door he jumped off the railing and headed toward me. His infectious grin had me smiling as well this time. I mean—we were getting ice cream!

"Have you thought about what flavor you're going to get?" he asked.

I shook my head. "You said they had a bunch of new ones, so I want to see what they've got."

"You always say that and in the end you always end up with Tiger Tiger," he joked, elbowing me in the ribs. I shrugged. I was a creature of habit and Tiger Tiger made me happy.

I listened to Chip talk about his latest video game and how he was "killing it" already. I only half listened, though, so I didn't immediately realize it when he'd quit talking. I looked at him questioningly to see what could have shut him up and found him looking down the back alley.

The Milky Way had both a front and back entrance, and it was the back entrance that had Chip's attention. His jaw was clenched, his fists balled at his sides. My gaze followed his and I saw what angered him.

A group of boys who looked to be our age were standing in a circle. At the center was a young boy wearing a baseball cap, obviously just come out of the ice cream shop, one double-scoop chocolate cone in his hand. He slowly turned inside the circle, a look of terror on his face. The boys forming the circle laughed and jeered at him, and every once in a while one would stick out a hand and try to grab his cone. He dodged the attempts, pulling his arm away, but

I could see that the ice cream was melting and starting to run down his hand. He looked near tears, trying to break out of the circle whenever he saw an opening, but the older boys wouldn't let him out

Chip strode purposefully toward the group and I quickly followed behind, afraid of how he planned to respond to this. As we got closer I heard the older boys taunting: "Give me your ice cream, Nathan!" and "You better give it to me or I'm gonna punch you!" I recognized Brady as the ring leader of the group, along with some of his usual pals. This wasn't the first time I'd witnessed Cody, Logan, Mason, and Dylan help Brady torment someone, but it was the first time I'd seen it up close—staying invisible always meant walking the other direction. As Brady took another swipe at the ice cream cone, Nathan jerked his arm back and both scoops fell to the ground with two successive splats. Nathan stared at them laying in the gravel of the back alley, and the tears spilled down his cheeks.

"Aw, now he's gonna cry 'cause his ice cream fell on the ground," Mason taunted, and the boys laughed. At that moment Chip reached the group, pushing Logan and Dylan aside and charging into the center to stand beside Nathan.

"Back off, Brady," he warned.

Brady's look of shock at Chip's appearance was gone just as quickly as it appeared. An evil smirk formed on Brady's face.

"And if I don't?" he asked.

"If you don't …" Chip growled, "I'm going to make you."

Brady laughed and elbowed Dylan. "Yeah, you and who's army?" he jeered.

"Just me," Chip responded, looking him in the eye and daring Brady to make a move one way or the other.

They stared at each other and I watched from a couple of feet away, frozen by my own fear. Dylan gave Chip a push from behind, making him take a couple of steps ahead toward Brady, who brought his fist up and into Chip's stomach. Chip doubled over.

My fear broke its hold on me. I ran toward him. When I reached the group I could see that Brady had punched Chip in the face because blood ran down his cheek from his eyebrow. Chip stood up and landed a blow to Brady's chin. As I saw Brady's fist come around again I made a grab for it. I missed and felt the force of his fist as it connected with my own cheek bone.

I fell to the ground and brought my arms up to cover my face in case Brady came in for another punch. Chip yelled. My vision blurred as I looked up to see two Chips flying toward Brady. Chip's fist connected with Brady's nose with a sickening crunch followed by a gush of blood. Brady reached up to wipe away the blood, his eyes narrowed. He started toward Chip.

Suddenly, I heard: "Hey, what's going on out here?" and I recognized the voice as George, the owner of the Milky Way. The next thing I heard was the scuffle of gravel as five sets of feet ran to the mouth of the alley.

I sat up and looked around. Chip was bent over, talking to Nathan, and George scowled at the retreating backs of the five boys.

"You all right, Hannah?" Chip asked as he consoled Nathan, who was clearly still upset. Nathan looked forlornly at his cone and the ice cream that was now melted in the dirt on the ground.

"Fine," I replied, but when I tried to get up I rocked back, dizzy. Chip grabbed my arm and helped me to my feet. An intense pain pulsed from my cheek.

"You kids okay?" George hollered. Chip nodded his head and George went back into his store. I dusted the dirt and stones off my shirt and pants.

"You still up for a cone?" Chip looked at me, then the little boy. "How about you, Nathan? Want to try again?"

Nathan's expression went from sadness to adoration as he nodded his head. As we walked to the store entrance, Chip looked at the side of my face.

"You're probably going to end up with a black eye," he observed.

"Probably," I agreed.

My eyes adjusted to the dim light as we entered through the back door of the store. Chip directed Nathan and I to a table and walked over to the counter. He grabbed a couple of napkins from the dispenser and dabbed the blood off his eyebrow while giving George our order.

"Three cones, George. A double-scoop of chocolate, the same of Tiger Tiger and Chocolate Chip Cookie Dough."

As George made each cone, Chip delivered them to our table. Nathan's tears finally dried as he licked his cone, all smiles. When Chip went back for his cone and reached into his pocket to pay, George held up his hand and said, "It's on the house," and he closed the lid to the ice cream cooler with a bang.

"Thanks, George," Chip said, lifting up his cone in a salute.

The three of us sat silently, enjoying the ice cream. My cheek stung each time I lapped at my cone, but it didn't stop me from enjoying the creamy goodness.

"Does your face hurt?" Nathan asked me, looking worried.

"Nah, I'll be okay," I told him. His look told me he didn't believe me. I gave him a weak smile, but it didn't seem to help.

"Thanks for helping me, Chip," he said.

"No problem, buddy. I would have done the same for anybody."

And I knew he meant it. Chip didn't back down when he saw an injustice being done. I, on the other hand, froze in fear. This wasn't the first time that I'd encountered a bully, but it was the first time I'd come to someone's rescue.

"What are you going to tell your mom?" I asked Chip.

He shrugged his shoulders and continued eating his ice cream, thinking. Then he said: "I'll tell her I got hit during a floor hockey game at lunch."

I wasn't convinced she'd believe that. I'd never seen anyone end up with an injury like that from floor hockey, but what did I know?

Some parents believed anything.

"What about you? You going to tell your parents what happened?" he asked as he crunched into his cone.

"No way," I answered. "They would just get all worked up. Just more problems."

"So what are you going to tell them? You're gonna have quite the shiner tomorrow."

"I'll tell them I got elbowed in gym during a basketball game." I borrowed his scenario and gave it a twist of my own. Chip snorted at my story. After the incident during noon activities a couple of weeks ago, he knew the chances of me playing basketball any time in the future were slim to none.

The thought of the lunchtime basketball incident was spoiling my ice cream. I decided to change the subject.

"Brady and his crew aren't going to be happy about you stepping in and defending Nathan. And Brady isn't going to let that punch in the nose go, either."

Chip nodded, but looked unconcerned.

By this time, Nathan had finished his ice cream cone. He got up from his chair and looked at Chip and me.

"Thanks for helping me out," he said shyly. Chip raised his fist and gave Nathan a bump. Nathan ran out the back door and Chip and I were left alone.

"I don't know whether to tell you that was a great thing you did today or tell you you're crazy," I started, "but I'm glad you did it."

"Well, thanks for sticking your face in at the right time. Chances are they would have pounded me into the dirt if you hadn't." He smiled. "I don't think I could have held my own five against one."

"I'd better get home." I rose and picked up the garbage on our table, putting it in the receptacle. We headed for the front door of the shop, not wanting to have another confrontation if Brady and his gang had returned and were waiting in the alley for us. We walked down the street and when we turned the corner to go home, I took a quick glance down the back alley. No one was there. I breathed a sigh of relief.

"Don't worry, Hannah, those jerks aren't going to do anything," Chip reassured me. I smiled, not convinced. I'd seen how they operated over the years—I highly doubted they would let this one lie.

* * *

As Chip predicted, my parents were alarmed when they saw my face that night at supper. Correction: my *mom* was alarmed. My dad barely responded, and probably wouldn't have noticed if my mom hadn't brought it up.

When I got home I grabbed an ice pack out of the freezer and went straight to my room. I had a royal headache thanks to Brady's punch to my face. I hoped the ice pack would bring down the swelling that was starting under my eye. When my mother called me for supper, I stopped to check my eye in the bathroom mirror. The swelling hadn't gone down any—in fact, it looked worse.

I slid into my chair at the dining room table, swinging my hair to the side of my face to cover up what was now a purpling bruise on my left cheek. I kept my head bowed over my bowl of chili and began to eat. I may have even gotten away with it if it hadn't been for my dad asking me to pass the basket of buns to him. I looked up and reached to my left at the same time that my mother reached for the butter. She took one look at my face, dropped her knife, and put her hands to her mouth.

"Hannah, what on earth happened to your face?" she asked incredulously.

My dad swung his gaze to me and frowned, squinting to get a better look at my face. It was then that I noticed my dad's eyes—the pupils were huge beneath drooping eyelids. He looked half asleep.

"Where'd you get the black eye?" he asked. He talked slowly, like he was taking his time to pronounce each word.

"Basketball game in gym today," I explained. I didn't offer any more information.

My mom jumped from her chair and came around to my side of the table. Pushing my hair back from my face, she looked closely at my cheek.

"How did you end up with a black eye from basketball?"

"Trudy had the ball and I was standing behind her. Stephanie tried to get the ball from her and when she moved the ball out of the way her elbow hit my cheek."

Mom continued to inspect my cheek, silent. Eventually, she let go of my hair and sat down at her place again.

"After supper, get some ice on that," she advised. "Or you're going to have a shiner for quite a while."

I nodded, relieved that the subject appeared to be closed. For a brief moment I tasted guilt for my lies, and the thought occurred to me to tell my parents what happened today at the Milky Way—but then it passed. I had a rule for this, and like all my rules, I refused to break it.

* * *

This wasn't the first time that I'd been pushed around by bullies. When I was younger I was a victim, just like Nathan. And just like now, I didn't breathe a word of it to my parents. I wasn't entirely sure why. Fear of what would happen was probably the right answer, but I was also afraid it might just make it worse.

In grade three, a couple of boys used to chase me home from school. Every day was the same. I'd leave the school yard to walk the two blocks home and Danny and Kim Luke would follow me on their bikes. They'd say things to me that I couldn't remember now, but I did remember being scared. It got so bad that I would wait inside my classroom until I hoped that they were gone, making excuses to my teacher, Mrs. Thornhill, that I was waiting for my cousin to come pick me up. Sometimes Mrs. Thornhill would let me clean desks or shelves in her classroom so I didn't have to go home right away. Mrs. Thornhill never let on that she knew why I didn't want to go home, she just let me stay and help. At the end of the year she gave me a beautiful bracelet for all the work I did for her. I felt guilty accepting the bracelet, because she didn't know that my help was really just a way for me to avoid the bullies that harassed me every day, my way of giving her something back for saving me all those days after school.

I never told my parents about Danny and Kim. I was scared and ashamed to tell them what was happening each day. Instead, I looked after it myself. I let them believe that everything was fine. And they did. From that moment on I kept my troubles to my-self—Rule #3—and slowly started to disappear some more.

CHAPTER NINE

The next morning I woke up and stumbled to the bathroom. The first thing I did was check my eye in the mirror over the sink. I groaned as I saw the purple ring that surrounded my left eye. I admired the purple tinges on the edge, but grimaced at the dark black color closer to the eye. My eyelid was still swollen despite the cold compresses I put on it last night.

I sighed. How would I cover this up? Makeup wasn't going to cover the bright purple or the black. It may have worked in a day or two, but not today. I hung my hair over my left eye. Nope—that wouldn't work either. Knowing me, I'd end up running into a wall and look worse than I did now.

Sunglasses! I raced to my room, rummaging through the junk on my dresser. I tried to remember the last time I saw them, which had to be weeks ago, but where I put them after that I had no idea. I opened the top drawer to my dresser and rummaged through the odds and ends mixed in with my clothes. Sometimes if I left my drawer open, the overflow of junk on top ended up inside my drawer. I pulled clothes out and searched underneath. Nothing! Thinking they must have been downstairs, I pulled on jeans and a sweatshirt, ran a brush through my hair, and took my search to the rest of the house.

I searched through everything on the kitchen counter. I found bills, magazines, receipts, and coupons—but no glasses. My last hope was the junk drawer. I pulled it out and immediately found my glasses sitting on top of the phonebook. I slipped them into my backpack and grabbed a bowl and the cereal. I sat down at the kitchen table and poured milk over my cereal. My mom came in wearing her nurse's scrubs and poured a cup of coffee.

"How's the eye this morning?" she asked.

I pulled my hair back. She looked at it and winced.

"How does it feel? Because it looks terrible."

"Thanks," I said wryly. "It doesn't hurt, if that's what you mean."

She nodded, satisfied that even though I looked like I'd gone three rounds with a world champion boxer, I wasn't suffering.

"Dad get called out to work?" I hadn't seen him this morning. He was usually up and ready to go by now.

"Your dad's not feeling well this morning," Mom replied, not looking at me. I got the strange feeling that she wasn't telling me the whole story. I watched her as she went through the stack of mail I'd rifled through earlier looking for my glasses. I didn't think I ever remembered my dad missing a day's work in my life. Something wasn't adding up.

"Do you think he has malaria?" I joked, trying to get some response from my mom. She snorted, but still wouldn't look up.

"No, just some bug, I think," she replied, opening an envelope.

I stared at her, trying to figure it out. What was going on? When she still didn't look at me, I picked up my bowl and put it in the sink.

"I better get going," I said, throwing my backpack over my shoulder, and headed for the front door. I looked back at my mother on my way out to see her staring at the stairs that lead to the next floor. She didn't answer me. Probably didn't even hear me.

It was a sunny morning, thank goodness, so I dug my sunglasses out of my backpack as I made my way down the street to school. On the second block I saw Chip waiting for me on the corner. This was a first, but I was glad to see him. I was dreading walking alone to school today. When I got closer I hollered, "Hey!" and he turned to look at me.

"Hey, back," he responded. As I got closer I followed his gaze down the street. There was nothing there, but he was so focused on it before I arrived he hadn't seen me coming.

"How's your eye?" I questioned, coming to a stop before him. He turned his head so I could look at the cut on his eyebrow. It looked red and sore, but it really wasn't as bad as it was yesterday.

"How's yours?" he asked.

"Okay. Still swollen."

"Nice shades," he observed, giving me a small smile. I rolled my eyes behind my glasses but of course he didn't see that.

"Thanks," I said. "You here to walk me to school?"

He shifted from one foot to the other and stuck both hands in the front pockets of his jeans. "Yeah, I thought you could use some company."

I studied him closely, and just like my mother he refused to meet my gaze. What was up with everyone this morning? I sighed and turned toward the school.

It wasn't until we were within half a block of the front entrance that I saw them: Brady, Logan, Cody, Dylan, and Mason, standing at the bottom of the steps leading to the school. I glanced at Chip—he was looking in their direction as well.

"Is this why you were waiting for me at the corner?" I quizzed him. He glanced at me for a moment, then his eyes were back on the group at the bottom of the steps.

"Yeah, I was worried that they might have a welcoming com-mittee planned for one or both of us this morning," he answered grimly.

I adjusted my backpack on my shoulder, thinking that I might need to hit one of them with it if things went badly. When we got within ten steps of them, they turned and faced us.

Brady's nose had two wide strips of white tape over it. It wasn't straight anymore either, with a definite hook to the right. Their faces were blank, but I knew underneath there was tightly controlled fury. My stomach dropped—were we about to have a repeat of what happened at the Milky Way yesterday?

Chip and I stopped a few feet from the group and waited for them to make the first move. Brady came forward, stepping right in front of Chip, their noses almost touching—or they would if Brady's were still straight. Chip didn't flinch, just stared right back at Brady.

"This is a warning, *Toby*," he growled in his most intimidating voice. "This isn't over ... not by a long shot." He stared silently at Chip for a few moments, then he turned his gaze to me.

I gulped in a breath of air, waiting for him to threaten me as well. He said nothing, but the threat was implied: it wasn't over for me, either. Then he turned and joined his group again. They began to leave, but not before he pointed his finger at us and repeated "It's not over." As if they were one body, they climbed the steps to the school.

I let out the breath I was holding and turned to Chip. He didn't look scared, like I probably did—he was angry. He clenched his hands in fists at his sides, his face red and his breathing heavy. Taking a deep breath, he started up the stairs. "Idiots," he muttered. I followed behind him.

Anxiety plagued me most of the day. I continually scanned the halls during break, afraid of an ambush lying around each corner. In class, Brady shot daggers at me every time I raised my eyes from my desk, until I finally quit looking up altogether. But I could still feel him looking at me—the hairs on my arms stood up, and it felt like ants crawling across my skin. Every time someone said my name, which thankfully wasn't very often, I would jump. Mrs. Barkowski gave me a strange look in math class when she called on me to answer a question and I gave a yelp. I spent all of math listening to Chip tap his pencil on his desk behind me, painfully aware of Brady, two rows over, cracking his knuckles.

By lunch I was a nervous wreck.

Chip and I found our usual spot on the front lawn. Brady's group was on the far side of the grass from us, but rather than ignore us as they usually did, at least one of them was watching us at all times, like they were taking sentry duty. I took a few bites of my sandwich, but I gave up trying to force it down. Chip, on the other hand, attacked his sandwich like it did something to him and kept his attention focused on Brady. It appeared he couldn't shrug off his anger at their "idiotic behavior"—his words, not mine. His anger hadn't gone away from this morning. If anything, it'd gotten worse.

"Chip," I said, but he didn't hear me.

"Chip!" I repeated a little louder. He looked my way for a brief moment and then continued his surveillance.

"Chip!" I yelled it this time. He jumped like I'd startled him.

"What?" He directed his irritation at me. Like I hadn't said his name three times to get his attention. I was the one who should be irritated.

"Ignore them," I told him. "They're all talk and intimidation, anyway."

He raised his eyebrows.

"Hannah, those twits over there bullied a boy over an ice cream cone and then tried to beat me up! I'm not going to ignore that! And frankly, I don't understand how you can."

I gaped at his outburst, hurt. I knew what they'd done was wrong, of course, but I'd dealt with this before. Just ignore them and after a while they'll get tired of you and move on to someone else. When faced with a confrontation, I avoided it every time. It just was not worth the fight for me.

"What are you going to do?" I asked, worried about his response.

"For now, nothing, but if they try anything, I'm not going to back down."

That feeling settled in my stomach again. The one broiling there all morning. The one that told me this was far from over. All I could do was "wait for the other shoe to drop," as my mom would say. I packed up my barely bitten sandwich and threw it in the trash can. The bell rang, and we went to class.

CHAPTER TEN

A week had passed since the fight. My eye healed up nicely, now a dull green with a hint of yellow and the odd purple spot. School was the same. Chip and Brady continued to dance around each other. They weren't openly hostile, but stared each other down constantly. I was still on pins and needles, afraid that the minute I let my guard down Brady would get revenge in some way or another. Add to this the strange behavior of my parents and I was pretty stressed out. If all that drama over my hug with Chip and my basketball accident and my poem hadn't died down, I don't know what I'd do. As it was, I couldn't sleep and that fluttering feeling had set up shop in my stomach. As a result, I wasn't eating and I couldn't focus at school because my mind jumped back and forth between my dad and Brady, Dad and Brady, Dad and … I missed two math assignments and bombed a science lab. My grades started to reflect my preoccupation with the events in my life.

My dad only missed that one day of work—which was still out of character for him—but that weird vibe in the house persisted. My mom was more distracted than usual and Dad moved through his days robotically. I didn't say anything, afraid that a comment could upset the mood of the house and bring in a tornado from the events that I wasn't aware of.

Saturday found me sitting in front of the television watching *The Hunger Games* for the fourth time. A book lay open, neglected, in my lap. I'd woken up at nine o'clock to the sound of my dad cranking up the lawn mower. I ate my frozen waffles alone. Dad was outside and Mom was catching up on her sleep after a double shift. I cleaned up my dishes, threw a load of dirty laundry in the washing machine, and sat down in front of the television for some mindless entertainment. It felt good having some time to myself without the constant stressful worry about what I'd find when I walked around a corner or what would be hanging on my locker in the morning. The house was quiet except for the murmur of the television and distant hum of the lawn mower.

Near the end of the movie the lawn mower's engine quit and the back door slammed. A cupboard door opened and closed, then another. I could hear liquid being poured into a glass and a top being screwed back onto a bottle. I said nothing, only listened. Then the glass clinks into the dishwasher and the back door closes again.

My heart rate had sped up and that weird fluttering was back in my stomach. I couldn't remember a time that my dad needed a drink to get through a Saturday, especially before noon. The lawn mower started up again. I stared at the television screen without seeing what was happening. I ran my hands through my hair, recalling meeting my dad at the house during lunch and him having a drink then, too. My mind posited possible explanations: he was stressed at work, he wasn't getting along with Mom, I disappointed him by skipping school, or something happened on that last call. All the possibilities ran through my mind. The thought that kept running over and over in my head was *Why is he drinking during the day?*

The frustrating part was that there was no way I could talk to my parents about this. I couldn't think of any way to casually ask the question, "So, Dad, I noticed that you're drinking during the day. What's up?" I learned long ago that there were certain topics that you don't ask your parents about.

I kept my questions to myself and tried to focus on the movie. I wasn't successful.

CHAPTER ELEVEN

Things at school were relatively quiet for a couple of weeks. Brady and Chip seemed to have moved on from the ice cream incident, back to barely tolerating each other's existence. Chip was back to his motto: "They're all just idiots, Hannah." I started to breathe freely again, not looking around every corner or jumping at every noise. The whole experience seemed to have been put in the past—which was fine by me.

Miss Thomas rounded her desk and clapped her hands together. She had a smile on her face, which was always a sure sign that she was about to say something we weren't going to like.

"All right, class, let's settle down," she commanded, and the small pockets of conversation around me stopped. She scanned the class to make sure she had our attention.

"Right!" She clapped her perfectly manicured hands again. Another sign we were going to hate what was coming. She began, "I want to tell you about something I did this weekend. A friend and I went to the city and attended a writer's café. Does anyone know what this is?"

She scanned the classroom again, looking for hands raised, but there was nothing. Everyone looked at her with a blank stare.

"No? Okay, a writer's café is a place where writers—obviously—come to share their poetry or stories, and other people come to enjoy coffee or tea and listen to them."

I got that feeling in my stomach again, afraid I knew where this lecture was headed. That sparkle of excitement glinted in her eyes—you know, the one that teachers get when they think they've happened on this really cool idea that will motivate students, but never does.

Miss Thomas's smile grew.

"We listened to five different poets and authors, and while we were there I got this great idea! This is something we should do in class! Each of you can write a piece and then we can invite your parents or guardians to come to our own 'writer's café' to hear your creations!"

Almost at once, like a choir, the class groaned a cacophony of sound around the room. I heard different phrases muttered, like "She's got to be nuts!" and "No way am I doing that!" and "Forget it, Miss Thomas."

A frown now replaced the smile that had been there only seconds ago, and her shoulders slumped momentarily. She took a breath and pasted the smile back on her face, now through clenched teeth, and she straightened her shoulders.

"Class! Class! Class!" Even after calling out and clapping three times, a number of people still muttered to themselves or to the person beside them

"This is not up for discussion," she explained. "Each of you will write a piece to present at our own writer's café in two weeks. It's going to be awesome! We'll have drinks and baked goods for the parents and they'll get to hear each one of your original works."

There was no groaning this time. Brady scoffed to himself and continued scribbling on his notebook. Trudy's arms were by her sides and for a moment she looked like she was in shock. Then she picked up her pencil with a look of acceptance and wrote what I assumed was the assignment due date in her book. I looked over at Chip. He stared straight ahead, seemingly unaffected by Miss

Thomas's announcement. Panic overwhelmed me and I felt the blood leave my face. At the front Stephanie waved her hand in the air enthusiastically.

"Yes, Stephanie," Miss Thomas asked before Stephanie dislocated her shoulder.

"Yes, Miss Thomas," Stephanie started, giving a small smile. "First, I love this idea! My question is, can we only submit one piece to read?"

I rolled my eyes. Of course, suck-up Stephanie wanted to submit more than one.

"Good question, Stephanie," Miss Thomas replied, "but because of time constraints I will have to limit you to only one submission."

Stephanie harrumphed and sat forward in her desk.

"Any more questions?" Miss Thomas asked. Everyone remained silent, so she clapped her hands again.

"All right, so the topic of your poem or story needs to deal with the theme of *identity*—what a person believes themselves to be. For the next two weeks we are going to look at how to write poetry and stories so that you can apply it to your pieces. So, for tomorrow I want you to have some idea of what you want to write about."

No one acknowledged her instructions except for Stephanie, who appeared to be making a list of possible topics to write about. It looked like her list was half a page long already.

"That's your homework for tomorrow. Good luck!"

I stuffed my books into my backpack. I noticed my writing notebook tucked inside. Up until Brady had read from it, it was my secret. Since he'd read from it, my backpack never left my sight. I thought about Miss Thomas's assignment. It wasn't the writing of the poem that had me panicking; it was the topic, and having to read it in front of a group of people. Put the two together and my mind went blank.

Chip met me in the hallway.

"So you don't seem too worked up over this assignment," I observed. He glanced at me before dodging out of the way of a herd of sixth graders running down the hallway.

"Meh, doesn't sound difficult. She didn't specify length or type of poem, so that means I could write a haiku or limerick. I figure all I need to do is dedicate a good half hour to the assignment and I'll be done. Also, the shorter the poem, the less time on stage reading it."

I chuckled to myself. Chip had it figured out already. I pictured him writing his poem tomorrow and spending every day for the next two weeks doing nothing in class, which I was sure would not go over with Miss Thomas. I could never chance having her breathing down my neck like that, no matter how good I was at disappearing into the woodwork.

"Well, I'm glad you have it all sorted. I have no idea what to write about. Identity? What does that even mean?" I shook my head.

"Who you are as a person?" Chip suggested.

"And who is that?" I shot back.

"Let's start with the obvious. You're a girl. You're in seventh grade. You like to write. You hate basketball," and he had the nerve to laugh. "You defend your friends. Those are all things that are part of your identity."

I considered what he said. I could definitely write about myself in those terms. With a thankful smile, I followed him outside for lunch, ideas already forming in my head.

CHAPTER TWELVE

"The guidelines for your writer's café assignment are on this sheet. Please do not lose them."

Amy passed the pages over her shoulder to Alex, who passed them to me. I quickly scanned the sheets. What I saw made my heart drop. The requirements for the assignment burst my bubble of motivation that I'd had up until this moment. To start with, our piece must be no more than twenty-five lines long if it was a poem, or three pages for a story. No longer. That, I was sure, was for Stephanie, who would likely write a novel if given the chance. Secondly, because the topic was about ourselves, it had to contain some information that no one else knew about us. Finally, it had to be written in free verse. Well, that was a relief. Unlike Chip, I had no desire to write haiku or limericks. I looked over to see his reaction to the requirements for the poem. Gone was the indifferent look from yesterday—today Chip looked the picture of panic. All the color had drained from his face and sweat was forming on his brow. If *Chip* looked panicked, I couldn't imagine how *I* must have looked.

He took the sheet of paper and slammed it down on his desk with his palm. I felt his frustration—it matched my own—but now we were stuck together. In fact, as I looked around the class, Chip's response mirrored that of most of my classmates. Except for

Stephanie, who looked so disappointed I thought she might cry.

Miss Thomas ignored us all and went over each of the requirements, answering questions, of which we all had many. Brady, however, was drawing on his sheet, oblivious to Miss Thomas's explanations.

"Let's make sure everyone is clear about what is expected for this assignment," Miss Thomas went on. "You're writing a short story of no more than three pages"—and she looked pointedly at Stephanie, who threw out her bottom lip in a pout—"or a free verse poem of no more than twenty-five lines." She paused for questions, but there weren't any. She went on.

"The topic is your identity. You need to write about something that no one knows about you. It may be something you value, a dream you have, a painful experience, or a strong belief you hold. Don't write about your favourite hobby or the best trip you've been on. I want to know about you and the person you are."

"Can I write about my dog? I value my dog!" Logan yelled out.

"Not if you're going to tell me what a great dog he is, but if you talk about how you value him as a companion, then yes. Trudy?"

"What about friends?" She smiled at Stephanie.

"Like I just explained to Logan, if you're going to tell me all about your friends and what fun you have, no." Trudy's face fell. "However, if you want to write about their kindness, generosity, compassion, go for it. Any more questions?"

When no one put up their hand, she began her lesson on choosing a topic. She showed us how to brainstorm ideas, then left us to come up with our own.

Chip's pencil hadn't moved since her lesson finished. I gave him a questioning look and mouthed, "What's wrong?" He just shook his head and resumed staring into space. I turned back to my own brainstorms, looking at what I had so far.

Last night, I went through my writing notebook to see if I had anything in it that would work for the assignment. I rejected them all because they revealed too much about me, which broke one of my rules. The list in front of me now was short: kind, quiet, and studious. The problem was, were those necessarily things that nobody knew about me? I wasn't convinced. What was the one thing that I'd be comfortable writing about myself that no one else knew? I had no idea.

When Brady read from my notebook, the whole school found out something I would never reveal about myself. They didn't know why I wished I was different, but I didn't want to enlighten them either. Everything in my notebook was for my eyes only.

My mind drew a blank. I absently tapped my pencil against my notebook. My head rested on my hand like a boulder. Suddenly, I felt like someone was staring at me. I looked up to see everyone around me giving me a dirty look. Miss Thomas stared pointedly at my pencil and I quit tapping. I blushed, glancing at the clock hanging over the door. Fifteen minutes remained in class—the last time I checked it had been twenty, and that seemed like an hour ago. My gaze wandered around the room, flicking over the motivational posters Miss Thomas hung everywhere. *Falling down is part of life—so is getting up!* and *Yes, I can!* mocked me from the walls of the classroom. I snorted to myself. Her motivational phrases did nothing to convince me that I should reveal anything about myself to the people sitting around me. As I scanned the room again my eyes focused on the list of rules posted on the bulletin board at the front of the class. I studied them. Let their meaning sink in. *Respect others. Respect school property.* They were nothing like the rules that I followed. These rules were for getting along, creating a "school community," as Miss Thomas called it. My rules were for self-protection. To keep me from getting hurt. They were my cloak of invisibility, just like in *Harry Potter.* They allowed me to move through my world with no one noticing me. A seed of an idea formed in my head and I scribbled "Rules" at the top of my page. The bell rang and I looked at the clock. Where had those last fifteen minutes gone? As I put my writing notebook in my backpack I noticed that Chip still sat with a blank piece of paper.

I stopped at his desk. "No ideas?"

He scowled at me and shook his head. Closing his notebook, he took his backpack off the back of his desk and shoved his books inside.

"Not so easy now, eh?" I asked, wanting to give him a hard time—it was rare to find something that stumped Chip for once.

"Nope, but I'll figure it out," he promised.

Miss Thomas gave us a big smile as we passed her desk on the way out. Neither of us returned it.

"Why did she have to go and put all those requirements on the assignment?" Chip complained.

"For precisely the reason you thought you had the assignment in the bag with half an hour of work," I said.

He grunted as we arrived at our lockers. Throwing his books inside and slamming the door, he proclaimed, "Well, it sucks!"

I couldn't disagree with him, so we headed out to our regular spot for lunch. Brady and his gang were over in their spot and ours was as far away as possible. We ate our lunch in silence for a few minutes and then I listened to Chip talk about the local baseball team and the game they had won the night before.

We hadn't been paying any attention to Brady's group until a football landed a few feet from us. Chip and I both looked at it like it might explode, when Dylan ran over and picked it up.

"Losers," he remarked, tossing it to Mason on the other side of the lawn.

"Jerk," I muttered as he jogged away.

Five minutes later the ball landed next to us again. This time Chip picked it up.

"Toss it here, loser," Dylan taunted.

Chip made to toss it to him and instead sent it sailing over Dylan's head to where Brady was standing. Brady was busy talking to

Cody and didn't see the ball coming. It hit him in the chest and bounced to the ground.

Brady looked around to see where the ball came from, and when he saw Chip standing with a smile on his face, he started toward us. He looked like he was ready to throw a punch at Chip again, but Dylan threw his arm up to block him.

Brady turned to Dylan and growled, "What are you doing?"

Dylan nodded to the front door, where Mr. Lucas had just come out. The teacher glanced around the groups assembled on the lawn. When his eye caught Dylan with his arm in front of a murderous-looking Brady, he lifted his eyebrow questioningly. Brady stepped away from Dylan and shrugged his shoulders.

Once Mr. Lucas had walked away, he looked squarely at Chip and said, "That wasn't very smart, *Toby*. I'll be waiting for you," and he spun on his heel to join his group. Dylan gave Chip a meaningful look and followed.

"Do you really think it's a good idea to keep poking him like that?" I asked.

Chip looked down at me and smiled before taking his seat on the grass again.

"But it's so much fun," he replied, grinning.

I rolled my eyes. I had no idea what Brady meant when he said "I'll be waiting for you," but I was sure that, whatever it was, it didn't mean good things for Chip. Chip, however, didn't seem concerned by the threat and continued to eat his lunch as if nothing happened. I shook my head at his self-satisfied smile.

When the bell rang I slowly started to pack up what was left of my lunch. If I took my time, maybe Brady and his crew would be in the school already. Chip was packed and waiting for me.

"Hannah, let's go. What's the hold up?"

"Nothing, can't I put my stuff away?"

He looked toward the door. "At the rate you're going, we're gonna be late."

Mr. Lucas was holding the door open as students filed in from the lawn. I breathed a sigh of relief and quickly finished stuffing my lunch away. Brady was standing near the door—he was definitely waiting for us to walk by. Mr. Lucas had different ideas, telling Brady to get to class. Brady shot a last, withering stare in our direction and trudged inside.

We were the last to arrive at the door, and Mr. Lucas seemed to be unaware of the current of anger running between Chip and Brady. We walked through the door and it closed behind us. Mr. Lucas followed us down the hall to our lockers. Across from us Brady leaned against his locker waiting for the bell to ring. When he spotted us round the corner he pushed off his locker toward us with a smirk on his face. At the sight of Mr. Lucas, who was still behind us, the smirk disappeared and Brady immediately changed direction, heading to class. Mr. Lucas gave us a quick, oblivious smile and headed into his classroom.

"Yeah, I think that you're going to find out what he meant by 'I'll be waiting for you' sooner rather than later," I said.

"He can bring it," Chip answered. I threw my backpack in my locker and pulled out my gym clothes. We headed to Mr. Cooper's class for attendance before going to the gym.

In the gym, Coach Sanders had gymnastics equipment set up around the room. *Great,* I think to myself, *we're going to do circuits for gymnastics.* My gymnastic ability amounted to being able to do forward and backward somersaults correctly, cartwheels that resembled drunk starfish, and occasionally holding a headstand for three seconds. Around the gym I saw mats, a vaulting box, springboard, and some other equipment I had no idea how you use. Oh, and the ropes were down, which meant I'd have to try climbing them. My record on the ropes: about a foot off the floor.

"Line up over here," Coach Sanders called.

The class shuffled up to the black line of the basketball court.

Coach Sanders stood in front of us with his hands on his hips.

"Safety is a priority when using this equipment. If you feel that a station or exercise is beyond what you can do, modify it or move on to one you feel more comfortable with. Five minutes at each station. Any questions?" He barely left any time to see if any of us would raise a hand before continuing, "We'll break off into groups of three."

Coach moved down the line and counted us off. Chip, Alex, and I were a group. I felt relieved—Trudy was on my left, and being in a group with her would have been downright painful.

"Where do you want to start?" Chip asked us.

Alex, who wasn't much of a talker, pointed to the balance beam Coach Sanders set up. Our group made our way over, but there were already two groups ahead of us, since this was basically the easiest station. We each took turns walking across the beam, focusing on balancing.

Coach Sanders came over and observed us. When he concluded we'd pretty much mastered walking in a straight line, he barked, "Speed it up!"

Chip, like an American Ninja, immediately picked up his pace, practically leaping across. Alex put one foot up on the beam, arms teetering. He started down the beam faster than he had previously, but near the end I could see him tilting to the left, and he fell off the bench. Brady, Mason, and Dylan, at the station ahead of us, saw Alex fall and grabbed their stomachs, bending over laughing at Alex lying on the floor. They elbowed each other in hysterics, then went back to their station. I leaned over and stretched my hand out to Alex. He grabbed it and climbed to his feet.

"You okay?" I asked.

He glared at the floor, avoiding my gaze, his face red. "Fine," he said, turning away. I shot a disgusted look at Brady and his group. He ignored me, even though he was looking right at me.

Before I could get up on the balance beam and take my own turn, Coach Sanders blew his whistle.

"Move, people," he instructed.

We rotated to the next station: somersaults. This I could do!

We were just finishing up five sets of forward somersaults when we heard a crash. The whole class paused to see Brady grabbing his ankle while Dylan and Mason looked on. Brady rolled around on the floor writhing in pain, holding on to his ankle, as Coach Sanders rushed over.

"What happened?" Coach asked as he straightened out the leg Brady had clutched to his chest. He gently touched Brady's ankle, but at the slightest movement Brady cried out in pain.

"I was getting off the vault box when I landed wrong and twisted my ankle. I can't move it!" Brady whined, seeming to be in a lot of pain. Coach Sanders slowly lowered his foot to the mat.

"We'd better get you checked out. Mason. Dylan. Take Brady down to the nurse and have her look at his ankle. Tell her to let me know what she thinks."

Mason and Dylan each grabbed one of Brady's hands and hefted him to his feet. He kept his injured foot off the floor, wrapping an arm around each of their shoulders. They slowly made their way out of the gym.

Coach Sanders looked around at the rest of the class and hollered, "Okay, show's over. Back to your stations."

We resumed our somersaults, backward this time, until the whistle blew again. We skipped the vault boxes—there was no way I was getting on that thing. We moved on to the ropes, where Chip scurried to the top, effortlessly, and I, as predicted, managed a single foot off the ground. Alex made it halfway up.

We spent the rest of the period avoiding or half-heartedly attempting each of the stations. When the bell rang to end class, I was relieved it was over.

I met Chip at our lockers to get our books for science. I was shocked to see Brady standing in front of his locker, looking fine. No crutches, and when he turned away he didn't even have a limp.

"He seems to have made a full recovery," I commented to Chip, who looked over my shoulder to see Brady walking down the hallway perfectly fine.

He frowned and contemplated Brady as he entered the classroom. "Weird. Why would he fake a twisted ankle?" he wondered aloud, giving voice to the thoughts rolling around in my head.

"I know. Those goofs love PE. They never miss." I continued looking at the spot where Brady disappeared into the classroom. I couldn't explain it—but I had a feeling that I may not want to, either.

I grabbed my backpack as the bell rang and Chip and I hustled off to science class. Today was our weekly unit exam, and I'd need every minute of class to complete Mr. Lucas's test. I slid my backpack under the lab bench just as Mr. Lucas placed the exam in front of me.

"Good luck," he encouraged, smiling. *He seems to take great delight in our discomfort,* I thought to myself, writing my name at the top of the page.

An hour later my hand was cramped, but I finished every question and checked my test over. I was confident that for the most part I'd done well. Chip, of course, finished ten minutes ago and was now flipping through his science textbook.

"One minute to finish up," Mr. Lucas informed us, and I grabbed my backpack from under the lab bench in anticipation.

The bell rang when the last person handed in their paper.

"What did you think?" Chip asked.

"Not too bad. I think I did pretty well on most of the questions," I replied.

We navigated through the crush of bodies making their way to the door. I felt a tug on my backpack and spun around.

"Oops, sorry," Mason said with a fake smile that said he really wasn't sorry at all. Dylan nudged him and they both laughed.

I grabbed the strap on my shoulder. Jerks. Once Dylan and Mason moved on, I took my backpack from my shoulder and checked to make sure the zippers were done up. They were. I sighed with relief, clutching the backpack, and followed Chip out the door.

Chip and I walked home together and went our separate ways two blocks from my house. My parents weren't home yet, so I went to the kitchen for a snack. On the counter sat a note from my mom asking me to start dinner. I got a frying pan and added the ground beef she left to thaw on the counter. As it browned, I chopped tomatoes and lettuce for tacos. I was just about ready to add the seasoning when she walked through the door.

She dumped her purse on the counter along with today's mail. "Oh, thanks, Hannah." She smiled tiredly as she pushed her sunglasses into her hair. "You don't know how much I appreciate you getting this all ready. I'm beat."

"Long day?" I asked as I stirred the meat.

"The longest," she said, sitting at the table and taking off her nursing shoes. "We had two accidents involving eight patients in total. Emergency was a nightmare all day."

I poured her a glass of iced tea and put it in front of her. She smiled and said, "Thanks," before taking a long drink.

Swallowing, she said, "Your dad called. He won't be home until later, so it's just you and me for dinner."

"Why won't he be home?"

"He had to stay at work. Some training or something," she said absently as she sorted through the mail.

I dished up our tacos and we ate while watching the news. My mom volunteered to do the dishes because I cooked dinner, so with my backpack in hand I retired to my room.

I turned on some music and sat cross-legged on the bed. I unzipped my backpack to get my writing notebook, thinking I should make another attempt to write something for my English assignment. I reached my hand into where I usually kept it toward the back and, with a rising sense of horror, realized it wasn't there.

I pulled my backpack into my lap and started frantically taking everything out. Pencil case, book, math textbook, notebook—but no writing notebook. I opened the front compartments, thinking I might have put it in one of them, knowing that I would never do that. Since Brady got a hold of it I'd diligently put my notebook in the same spot every day. My hands searched through each compartment, finding gum, a paper clip, and lip gloss, but my writing notebook was nowhere to be found.

I tossed my backpack on the floor and began going through the clothes laying on the floor, throwing each article over my shoulder, hoping that they'd reveal my notebook underneath. Clothes now everywhere—writing notebook nowhere. My heart sank. Where could it be? I stood with my hands on my hips and surveyed my room. The only other possibility was my desk, which was piled high with books and papers. I didn't think I'd touched anything on there since yesterday, but I rifled through every piece of paper and looked carefully between books.

No notebook.

I sank slowly onto my bed. All that kept running through my mind were three words:

Where is it? Where is it?

Over and over on a continuous loop.

I searched my room again and still came up with nothing.

"Hannah, our show is on! Come and watch," my mom called up the stairs.

"In a minute," I replied distractedly. I stood in the middle of my room, tears threatening to fall down my face as I considered the implications of losing my writing notebook.

"Hannah!" my mom called again.

I sighed and went downstairs. My mom was curled up on the couch, our weekly bachelor show running the opening credits. I sat in the recliner, staring at the television, my mind still going a mile a minute, running through scenarios that would reveal where my book was. The most terrifying being that someone at school had found it—and was reading it right now.

"Hannah, are you all right?"

"Huh?" I asked, startled by her question.

"You all right? You can't sit still and you aren't even watching the show."

"Oh, it's nothing." I wished I could tell her what was going on, but my mom knew nothing about my writing. This was a problem I would have to solve myself.

"You sure?" she questioned again.

"Yeah, just preoccupied with an English assignment," I lied.

She studied me for a moment. "Mmm hmmm," she said, then turned back to the show.

I inwardly breathed a sigh of relief, then instantly went back to worrying.

CHAPTER THIRTEEN

I was fifteen minutes earlier than usual for school the next day. Up until today, I usually timed my arrival with the first bell. Today, the hallways were eerily empty as I spun the combination on my locker. I yanked on the lock, but it didn't open. Again, I frantically twisted the combination of the lock, and this time when I gave it a rough pull it opened. I threw the door open and it banged against Chip's locker. I looked to see if the sound would bring anyone to check and see what the racket was in the hallway. When no one appeared, I started going through the books that lined the bottom of my locker. Twice. It wasn't there.

I tried to think about the last time I saw it. I knew it was in my bag yesterday because I had it during English class. My notebook was in my backpack when I stowed it in my locker for gym, but I couldn't remember seeing it after that.

I was still racking my brain to remember if I'd seen it after gym when Chip walked up. He must have noticed the panicked look on my face, because his mouth opened to say his usual "Hey," but "Hannah? What's going on?" came out instead.

I shook my head. Panic had stolen my voice.

He grabbed the door to my locker and looked at the mess inside. My locker was always neatly organized. "Did someone ransack your locker?"

I shook my head.

"Did you have another gift from Brady?"

I shook my head a third time.

"You're freaking me out right now, Hannah! What is it?" he demanded, his voice getting louder.

I swallowed, trying to get some moisture back into mouth.

"My writing notebook … it's gone," I squeaked out.

"Gone? What do you mean 'gone'?"

Frustration overcame my panic and I threw my hands out to the side.

"Gone! I had it yesterday after English and I put it in my backpack before gym. I don't remember seeing it again after that!" My voice rose louder and louder.

"Okay, okay," he reassured me, holding out his hands in a gesture meant to calm me down.

It didn't work. I threaded my hands into my hair, wanting to pull it out.

"I don't understand. I know I had it yesterday and last night I went to work on my English assignment and it wasn't there. I turned my bedroom upside down. Nothing. I just don't understand where it went."

My chest felt tight. I was panicking again.

"Breathe, Hannah," Chip said.

I took a shaky breath. Then another. Slowly my breathing came back to normal.

"Did you go through when you saw it last?" he asked. Looking at me tentatively, like he was afraid the answer would make me lose it all over again.

"*Yes!* I've gone over it a hundred times," I cried.

"I'll help you find it, just calm down," Chip said.

I nodded.

The bell rang. Students poured into the hallways.

I closed my locker and we turned to head to Mrs. Barkowski's math class. As we made our way to math, someone bumped my shoulder, jostling my backpack.

"Sorry, loser."

I looked up to see Brady's smarmy smirk. That was the second time in two days that I'd had someone run into me. And both times one of *his* gang.

Brady was already three steps past me when I realized what happened.

Brady bumped into my backpack.

Just like Dylan. Dylan bumped into my backpack yesterday, right after the last time I'd seen my notebook.

"Oh, no," I whispered.

* * *

I got nothing done in math. All I could think about was my notebook in Brady's hands, and when or where it would show up. I prayed that it was just misplaced somewhere and not in the hands of one of my classmates, but a part of me knew better. Thankfully Mrs. Barkowski didn't notice my preoccupation, which was great, but only left me more time to obsess about the whereabouts of my missing book.

I didn't hear the bell when it rang. I just sat in my desk after most of the class had left, until Chip hissed at me.

"Are you sure you're okay?" he asked as we rushed to English. I wasn't sure. My personal thoughts and ideas were in that book. Thoughts and ideas I'd never shared with anyone. A cold sweat broke out on my forehead just thinking about Brady reading them—and reading them out loud to who knew who else.

Miss Thomas talked about figures of speech in poetry, but I only listened with one ear. I jotted down the notes she put on the board mechanically, not paying attention. With twenty minutes left in the period she gave us the time to work on our writer's café assignments. I automatically reached for my writing notebook—and stopped when I realized it wasn't there, obviously. Wow, I must have been really out of it. For a minute I didn't know what to do. I just sat there, frozen, until Miss Thomas came by my desk.

"Problems, Hannah?" she asked.

I looked at the English notebook on my desk and opened it to a blank page.

"No, ma'am," I mumbled, picking up my pencil.

"Where's your brainstorming?" she asked when she saw my blank page.

"I think I left it at home?" I knew it shouldn't sound like a question, but that was the way it came out.

She looked down her nose at me disapprovingly. "You know you're going to get time each class to work on this assignment, Hannah. You need to be prepared."

"Yes, ma'am." Out of the corner of my eye I saw a look pass between Brady and Dylan. They then looked at me and gave me their trademark smirk.

I tried to remember what was on my brainstorming list, but I could only remember two topics. While I struggled with my list, Miss Thomas stopped at Brady's desk. She asked him about his chosen topic—and my heart dropped when I heard his reply.

"I think I'm going to write about courage, Miss Thomas. I'm not sure if people know what a courageous guy I am," he told her.

"Oh, I like that, Brady," she said approvingly.

Courage? Oh, no. Oh … no.

The poem I wrote the morning I skipped class was about courage.

My suspicions were right. I was certain now.

Brady somehow got his grubby hands on my writing notebook!

He and Miss Thomas exchanged comments for another moment before she moved on to the next student. Brady turned around and gave me a knowing look.

My panic suddenly drained away. Now I was furious. I couldn't believe he would steal my work and pass it off as his own. I tried to imagine any number of ways that I could bring him bodily harm. But then I realized—I wouldn't do anything. If I confronted Brady, I was sure his response would be to show my pieces to anyone and everyone. I put my head on my desk as the reality of it washed over me.

Chip poked me in the shoulder. I raised my head and looked at him.

"You okay?" he asked.

I shook my head, mumbling that I'd talk to him later.

The last ten minutes of class dragged by.

Chip caught up to me in the hall on my way to the gym.

"Okay, Hannah. Spit it out," he demanded.

I looked around at the students surrounding us. "I'll tell you at lunch."

Even though I could see he wanted to argue, he nodded his head and we went to gym. I was a little afraid of what would happen if I told Chip, but I knew I would. I just couldn't keep it inside any longer.

* * *

I made slow work of getting my lunch out when we got to our usual lunch spot.

"Spill," Chip stated, ignoring his own lunch and looking straight at me. I considered my sandwich, then threw it back in the container.

"So today in English I overheard Brady tell Miss Thomas that his poem for the writer's café was going to be about courage."

"Okayyy," Chip said, drawing that word out in confusion. "Why does that have you so upset?"

"Remember the day that I skipped out after he read my writing in science?"

"Yeahhh," he said, still not putting two and two together.

"Well, I spent the morning at the park and while I was there I wrote a poem about courage." I said it all in a rush, hoping to get the words out before I choked on them.

"So you think it was Brady that took your writing notebook?"

"After he told Miss Thomas what his poem was about he looked right at me and smirked," I answered.

"When would he have taken it?" he asked.

I knew he took it, but Chip was right—when would he have had the opportunity? I thought back for what seemed like the millionth time, and when it suddenly dawned on me, I became furious all over again.

"The day he got 'injured' in gym class," I ground out. "Dylan and Mason supposedly took him to the nurse, but afterward he seemed absolutely fine, remember? I think they used his *injury* as a chance to break into my locker and take my writing book. We know that they've just been waiting for a chance to get back at us after what happened at the Milky Way."

Chip nodded his head and then looked over his shoulder. Brady, with his back to us, lounged with his groupies in their usual spot. Before I could stop him, Chip was on his feet storming in their direction. When Chip reached their circle he shoved Brady from behind.

Brady whirled around. "What the …?" was all he got out before Chip shoved him again. Mason and Dylan tried to grab Chip's arms, but he slipped from their grasp and went after Brady again.

"You jerk!" he yelled. "You take her book and try to pass her writing off as your own? You're a thief and a dirt ball!"

Brady had his arms up to defend himself when I got there, along with a few other kids. Laughing, he said, "Man, I don't know what you're talking about. I didn't take anything from anybody."

"You stole her book out of her locker when you faked that twisted ankle," Chip said, pointing his finger at him.

"Get a grip, buddy," Brady said, shoving Chip back. "You better back off, or I'm going to give you another lesson like last time."

Instead of backing off, Chip went after Brady again. Dylan and Mason were pulling him off Brady when I pushed my way through the crowd gathered around them.

"Give the book back!" Chip growled out, lunging again.

"I told you, I don't have any book. You need to chill."

I yanked on Chip's arm and his head twisted in my direction. "Stop, Chip! It's not worth it. He'll never admit that he's got my book."

Brady snorted. "It's your book? Why would I take your book? A bunch of sad little poems about being different?"

Chip tried one more time to get his hands on Brady. I yanked on his arm again and he finally backed up, glaring across the circle.

"Come on," I said.

He finally quit pulling against my arm and walked backward, away from the group. The rest of the kids meandered off, now that the show was over. I led Chip back to our spot on the grass and listened as his breathing slowed down.

"It's him, Hannah! I know it," he bit out.

I understood Chip's frustration all too well. "I know! But, Chip, if I accuse him of taking my notebook, he's just going to reveal everything that's in it. The way it is now, he denies having it. If we take this any further he could plaster my thoughts and feelings all over the school," I stared Chip in the eyes, trying to show on my face how desperate I was to keep that from happening.

"I don't like it, Hannah," Chip said heatedly. "It's not right. He shouldn't be allowed to take your ideas and thoughts and use them for himself."

"Look at it this way. He's only got so many pieces of mine that he can use. I can always write more. He can't."

Chip gazed across the lawn in thought. I hoped I'd convinced him to let it go.

"Okay. But I still don't like it," he told me with a scowl on his face.

I was thankful to have Chip in my corner, but this was about self-preservation. I didn't want people to know that it was my work that Brady was passing off as his own. I was glad to have convinced Chip for now, but how long would this last?

We sat in silence until the bell rang.

CHAPTER FOURTEEN

We remained quiet on our walk home after school. Chip wasn't his usual talkative self, and I didn't dare to bring anything up, afraid he'd try to convince me to change my mind. In an effort to repair the rift between us, I made a suggestion.

"Hey, since it's Friday night, why don't we go see a movie?"

Chip didn't answer right away. I was afraid he would dismiss the suggestion since he was disappointed in me. But after a couple of minutes, he asked, "What's playing?"

Relieved, I told him that it was one of those new superhero movies, but I wasn't sure which one.

"Why not," he replied with no enthusiasm at all.

"Great!" I said, overly cheery to compensate. "Pick me up at seven?"

He responded with a "Sure" and we parted ways at our usual corner. I let myself in the house and looked for a note from my mom about dinner, but there wasn't one. Maybe she would get it ready when she got home.

I went up to my room, which still looked as if a bomb had gone off. The mess just reminded me that Brady had my notebook, so I spent time sorting through the clean and dirty laundry that littered the floor. When I finished that, I looked around for something else to do. Normally, I would get out my writing notebook and write, but that wasn't an option. I lay on my bed staring at the ceiling, going through the events of the day.

With a huff, I got up and dug through my desk to find a notebook. Once I found one, I didn't write anything on the front. I'd learned my lesson about advertising what was inside. I crawled on my bed and began to write. By the time my mom came home I'd written another poem. I put my book on my desk and climbed downstairs.

"Hey," I said as I came into the kitchen. My mom looked up from chopping vegetables and smiled briefly.

" 'Hey' yourself. How was your day?" she asked.

"You know, like any other," I told her. I didn't want her to ask a bunch of questions, so I changed the subject. "Where's Dad?"

My mom's face went blank. "Work," she said simply.

"He seems to be working a lot of overtime hours," I observed, and she nodded, saying nothing. No explanation. Weird.

The two of us ate dinner, and after dishes were done I told her that Chip and I were going to the movies.

"Okay," she said absently, sitting on the couch staring unseeingly at the television.

I went upstairs to change for the movie. The doorbell rang just as I turned off the light and headed downstairs. Chip was talking to my mom in the front entrance.

I grabbed my coat off the hook by the door. "Later," I said and closed the door.

Chip was quiet at first, but soon we were talking and joking like we always did. I felt a wave of relief that he was no longer upset with me.

The movie was a bust in my opinion. Chip, however, couldn't quit talking about the special effects—especially all the blood, which made me wonder if I would lose the popcorn and pop I ate during the movie. I was sure there must have been a greenish tinge to my face, but Chip was oblivious. When he took a breath to carry on his reenactment of his favorite parts, I finally managed to stick my hand out.

"Stop! If you go over one more gruesome scene, I'm going to puke right here," I informed him.

Shocked, he stopped and looked at me closely. "Oh, sorry," he replied sheepishly, laughing. I couldn't help laughing with him.

We walked in awkward silence for the next block. Chip picked leaves off the trees we passed, ripping them into tiny pieces. He seemed like he wanted to say something, but maybe he was afraid to for some reason. As we stepped off the curb he took a deep breath and I braced myself for whatever he was about to say.

"I know you don't want to talk about it, Hannah, but I really need to understand why you won't tell anyone that Brady stole your book," he said in a rush.

I sighed inwardly and glanced at his face. I saw both concern and confusion, battling each other in his eyes and in his arched eyebrows. It scared me to share the importance of my book with him—it went against all my rules. When he said nothing, just patiently waited with those imploring eyes, I inhaled a deep breath and started speaking.

"Chip, my writing notebook is the one place where I can be me. The real me. Not the invisible one. That book holds all my hopes, dreams, heartaches, and hurts. It is the one place I can be honest about my dad. Where I can share how deeply hurt I am when he ignores me or demands that I do things that he thinks are important. I can write about how frightened I am when he gets angry or how little he trusts me. That book is the one place I let down my guard and for someone to be able to read all my thoughts and feelings is terrifying. It's like pulling back the curtain and revealing myself to the whole world."

Chip stood quiet for a moment, considering my words. Then he spoke, and what he said surprised me.

"I know how you feel, Hannah. I know what it's like to have a difficult father. I wasn't totally honest with you when I told you about why I preferred the name 'Chip' over 'Toby.' I told you I despised the name because it was the same as my dad's—and that's the truth—but the reason I despise him is because for years before he finally left … he used to beat my mom."

My breath caught with his revelation. I put my hand on his arm to comfort him, but I knew it wasn't enough.

"Chip, you don't have to tell me this if it's too painful."

"No, I want to tell you. I want you to know that, despite your dad and all the other people who have hurt you, you are a great person and you don't need to try to be invisible—you need to be you. Hannah, you're kind, caring, funny, smart, and, I think, a terrific writer. You need to let that show—not for other people, but for yourself."

"You're pretty great yourself. Your dad—that's why you defended Nathan, right? And why you wanted to go after Brady for taking my book?"

Chip shrugged. "Pretty much."

I smiled at him. We walked two more blocks in silence, but it was no longer awkward. Even though I still worried about Brady having my notebook, I felt lighter knowing that Chip and I had so much in common.

I felt a little better by the time we reached the corner to go to our houses.

"Maybe talk to you tomorrow?" I asked.

"Yeah, maybe. Goodnight, Hannah."

I found my mom stretched out on the couch when I got home, the television on to some show about people living in Alaska. I'd never seen her watch it before, but maybe she had a sudden curiosity about living in isolation. I didn't see my dad's truck in the driveway and didn't mention it.

"Night, Mom," I called to her, and she mumbled "Goodnight" back.

I got ready for bed, confident in the knowledge that I would have some pretty vivid nightmares after seeing that movie—but after the week I'd had, any distraction was welcome.

CHAPTER FIFTEEN

I was pulled out of my restless sleep by Mom shaking my shoulder and shouting.

"Hannah, wake up!"

I tried to peel my eyelids open groggily. Clothes hit my face, but I was confused and still half asleep.

"Get dressed, Hannah," she barked as I pulled the clothes off my face and saw her heading toward the door.

"What's going on?" I demanded, propping myself on my elbows to look at her

"We have to go to the hospital. Get your clothes on!" I noticed she hadn't showered, her hair still crimped from sleep.

"The hospital? What? Why? Did something happen to Dad?"

"Your dad?" she asked, pausing. "Why would your dad be at the hospital?"

"I don't know," I deflected, not wanting to let on that I'd been worried about my dad's behavior lately. "Who else could it be that you're in such a panic?"

"It's Chip," she said.

Dread filled my body.

"Chip? Is he sick?"

My mom came back and sat on my bed, putting her hand on my leg.

"Hannah, honey, Chip was jumped on his way home from the movie. His mom called this morning to let me know. He's pretty badly beaten and I told her I'd bring you over to see him."

I was stunned. I searched her face to see some sign that she was joking, maybe, or that this was just a dream, but all I saw was fear and concern. When I realized that she was telling me the truth, that this was real, I threw back the covers and yanked my clothes on. I was ready in a minute and I raced down the stairs to wait impatiently by the door.

My leg jumped a mile a minute as we drove to the hospital. I stopped myself from telling her to drive faster because I wanted to get to the hospital like yesterday, and I also wanted to slow time down because I was scared of what we would find.

Mom parked in the emergency section and we ran across the parking lot. I was grateful my mom was a nurse—she knew exactly where to go to find Chip. When I pushed open the door to his room my breath left me in a rush and I stood still, blocking the doorway.

Chip lay on a narrow hospital bed, his left arm in a cast across his stomach. He turned his head to show both eyes to be black and blue, stitches over his right eye—but he still had that signature Chip smile on his face. My hand rose to my mouth. I tried to choke down a sob, but I couldn't.

Beside him, his mom Shelley sat in a chair. Dark circles under her eyes made her look like she hadn't slept all night. She gave us a tired smile and motioned us over. I took a few steps and I felt my mom right behind me. As I got close to Chip's bed my steps slowed, like I was afraid I'd hurt him if I got too close. My mom put a hand at the small of my back and pushed me forward. When I reached Chip's uninjured hand, I gently clasped it. I said nothing. I didn't know what to say. I looked at him as tears slid down my cheeks.

"How are things, Shelley?" I heard my mom say as I stood there, numb, looking at Chip.

Shelley sighed. "Well, they finally got his cast on. The X-ray showed it was broken in two places, so we had to wait until they decided the best way to cast it. He got five stitches over his eye, but it's his spleen they're worried about."

"His spleen?" I asked, confused.

"Two guys held my arms while the third one punched me in the stomach. I don't know how many shots I took, but they're worried it may have ruptured my spleen. If it did, then I'll have to have surgery." He smiled weakly. I noticed that his front tooth was chipped. His nickname suddenly took on a whole new meaning.

I couldn't comprehend what Chip was saying. Who punched him? Why?

"Who did this to you? Did the police catch them?" I asked, my voice rising.

"I don't know who it was, Hannah. I was walking past the back alley by our house after I left you on the corner. One minute I'm walking alone and the next I'm being punched and kicked. They were all wearing black, so I couldn't see who it was." Chip clenched his teeth in pain after his explanation and I patted his arm.

"So you called the police then?" I asked.

Shelley nodded. "Not that it's going to do much good. Chip can't identify them because they were dressed in black and they never said a word. Just beat him to a pulp." I could see she was upset, in her furrowed brow and grim mouth. She tried to hold back tears as my mom rubbed her back. "It seems like they knew he was going to be there and were waiting for him. Who would do such a thing?" she said.

Chip and I exchanged a look that said, "I know who," but we said nothing aloud.

Shelley wiped her eyes. "The police said they'd ask around, see if anyone saw anything, but I doubt if anybody will step up."

"When are you getting out?" I asked.

"They want to keep me a few days for observation, to keep an eye on my spleen and make sure it's not going to suddenly rupture,"

Chip said.

I nodded and looked at my mom. "I'm going to stay here for a while."

She looked at me and then at Chip. "Call me when you're ready to come home. I'll come back and pick you up. Shelley, why don't I drop you off at your place? You can have a nap and shower while Hannah's here to keep Chip company."

Shelley glanced at Chip questioningly and he nodded. "Go get some rest, Ma," he said. "Hannah will keep me entertained." He smiled and squeezed my hand.

Shelley picked her purse up off the floor and followed my mother. When they were gone, the door closed, I asked Chip the question I'd been holding back.

"Was it Brady and his crew?"

"It could've been. But I honestly don't know. It happened so fast, and then they were gone and I was laying on the sidewalk. I managed to get up and get to the house, and Mom brought me here. I've been poked and prodded every ten minutes since I arrived. I haven't had much time to go over it again."

Chip's eyes started to droop and I realized he had probably been awake most of the night. I told him to rest and took up my vigil in the chair next to his bed. I stared at the bruises on his face, thinking about what it must have been like to have three people beating on you, to be defenseless. Cuts and scrapes covered the knuckles on Chip's hand—he must have made an attempt to defend himself, at least.

I knew this was the work of Brady and his friends. Who else would want to hurt Chip like this? It was payback for the times he defended Nathan and me. I stifled the sob that rose in my throat. As I tried to control the sadness threatening to overwhelm me, I realized that I was also angry. Angry at Brady for thinking that he could bully and beat people. He treated people and their property with no respect. Angry that Chip, while trying to defend people from Brady, ended up in the hospital, beaten. My anger grew as I sat and tried to think of ways to make this better.

I spent the day with Chip, keeping him company when he was awake and watching him sleep as I plotted some kind of revenge. At one point Chip woke up and, seeing the scowl on my face, said, "Quit it, Hannah."

"What?"

He looked at me pointedly. "I know that look. You're trying to think of a way to get back at Brady. It's not going to work. Besides, I don't know for sure if it was him or not."

"I'm not," I denied, and he raised his eyebrows skeptically. I kept my face blank and held his gaze. "I'm not," I repeated, and after a moment of looking in my eyes he seemed convinced.

Chip drifted off to sleep and I spent that time thinking about our discussion the night before. The way Chip saw me wasn't the way I saw myself. I thought about our writer's cafe assignment and how we needed to write about something no one knew about us. And I made a decision.

I wasn't going to hide anymore.

Chip was right. I needed to show people who I really was.

CHAPTER SIXTEEN

I barely managed to drag myself out of bed Monday morning and get ready for school, I was so tired. My back ached from sitting in the hospital chair all weekend. My dad was drinking coffee at the kitchen table when I got downstairs. He looked like he hadn't sleep in the last few days either.

I hadn't seen my dad in a while. I spent all day Sunday at the hospital, too, and he wasn't home when I got up. My mom dropped me off early and she seemed preoccupied. She said he had an emergency call before I woke up, but I wasn't sure I believed her. Chip appeared better Sunday, and we spent time looking through the magazines I brought and playing tic-tac-toe.

"Morning," I said to my dad as I entered the kitchen.

He glanced up from the newspaper and gave me a small smile. "Morning," he replied.

"It seems like I haven't seen you for days," I told him.

He looked at his paper, not meeting my eyes. "Yeah, things have been hectic at work the last couple of days," he said to the news-paper.

I waited for him to add more, but he said nothing. I grabbed some breakfast, threw together a quick lunch, and let myself out the door.

School wasn't the same without Chip there. I was back to staring at the tops of my shoes as I walked down the hallways. Back to being Invisible Hannah. I didn't talk to anyone and they didn't talk to me. I hadn't realized until now what an important part Chip played in my life.

I got to English class after eating my lunch by myself on the front lawn. While I waited for class to start, there was a commotion in the doorway and I looked up to see Brady, Dylan, and Mason all fighting to get into class at the same time. I realized that this was the first I'd seen of Brady all day. He looked like his normal self. No bruises or cuts on his face. I inspected him closely as he sat down in his desk and joked with Stephanie. He must have felt me looking at him, because he brought his hand up and scratched the back of his head.

And that was when I noticed the cuts on his knuckles. The same cuts that I saw on Chip's knuckles. It took all the willpower I could muster not to fly across the aisle and attack him in the same cowardly way he attacked Chip.

He suddenly turned and looked right at me. I stared back, not afraid to meet his gaze now. I pointedly looked at his right hand. He hid it out of my sight in his lap. I continued to stare him down, but he averted his gaze, pretending not to acknowledge me.

The bell rang and Miss Thomas began her lesson on story structure. I wasn't listening. I was focused on Brady's knuckles—the evidence of Chip's beating. I didn't realize the lesson was over until she was standing by my desk.

"Where's your project, Hannah?" she asked. I looked at her and at first I didn't register what she was talking about. "Your writing?" she prompted. I blinked, then, realization dawning, reached for my notebook and opened it to the brainstorming sheet I started last week.

"That's all you have? You better get working, Hannah. Our writer's café is on Friday." And with that she moved on to the next person.

I sat looking at the list and then, with all the anger still raging inside me, I ripped the page out and crumpled it up. I looked at Brady once more before I began to write furiously.

CHAPTER SEVENTEEN

F riday.

I sat in English class. Our desks were pushed against the wall and chairs were arranged in a half circle around a podium that sat in the middle. Chip sat beside me—he'd been back to school for two days. He was released from the hospital on Monday and had been recuperating at home until yesterday. I'd been to his house every day to see how he was doing. We hadn't mentioned our conversation from the hospital. We watched television and ate the snacks that Shelley made us.

Chip peered at me when my leg started beating out a rhythm on the floor. He knew I was nervous, but he didn't know why. I gave him a weak smile. Parents sat quietly in a ring of chairs behind us. I didn't tell my mom or dad about the writer's café. They did question what I was up to all week, locked in my room, but telling them I was working on a project for school seemed to satisfy their curiosity.

I spent every evening working on how to find the best way to express what I wanted to say. I was going to reveal something about myself that no one knew, but I was also going to send a message. That I would be invisible no longer. That stealing my notebook and beating up Chip was the act of a coward and I wouldn't hide my anger at the injustice of it anymore. The floor of my bedroom was littered with the snowballs of paper that I crumpled up and threw there as I found the words that best described my contempt for Brady and his gang. It wasn't until late last night that I was happy with the words that I was about to say. But I was still so nervous every nerve in my body was screaming at me to run away.

Chip nudged my arm and I gave him a scowl. He lifted his chin toward the door. I turned to see my mom walk in. She found a chair in the outer circle and waved after she sat down.

I turned to Chip and hissed, "What's my mom doing here?"

Chip got a sheepish look on his face and said, "I may have told her that you were going to be reading a poem today for writer's café?" He said it like a question but I knew that he purposely told her. My dad wasn't with her, which didn't surprise me, and for that I was thankful.

"You're so dead when this is over," I told him through gritted teeth. It was the basketball game all over again. He smiled, opening his mouth to say something, when Miss Thomas cleared her throat at the front of the room.

She introduced herself and thanked all the guests for coming to hear our writing pieces. She then asked Stephanie to come forward—probably because Stephanie hounded her for the chance to go first for the last week.

I tuned it all out. With each student's performance, my mouth got drier and drier. The paper in my hand became damp and crumpled.

About half the class had gone and we were already running into science class when Miss Thomas called my name.

I jumped in my chair.

I slowly made my way to the podium at the front. I opened the folded paper and flattened it. I didn't look up. I cleared my throat, took a deep breath, and read the title.

" 'I See You,' by Hannah Williams," I read aloud.

Then I opened my mouth to start the poem itself—and nothing came out. I cleared my throat again.

"I see you,
King of your domain,
Lording yourself over those you see as weaker.
I see you,
Wreaking havoc with your minions,
Destroying everything in your path.
I see you,
Your smarmy smirk at others' pain,
Stealing whatever you want.
You don't see me.
You look through me, around me, over me,
Not worthy of your consideration.
I'm tired of your tyranny.
I'm tired of your indifference.
I'm tired of bending to your will.
I'm tired of being invisible.
It's time for you—
To see me."

As I prepared to read the last line of the poem, I raised my eyes to look directly at Brady. And as I read them—"To see me."—I knew he understood that it was directed at him. His face flushed a bright red. He got my message.

The room was quiet for a moment and then it broke out into applause. Chip stood, doing an awkward one-handed clap with his cast. My mom stood up as well with a bewildered look on her face. I looked around the room—my classmates were all smiling and clapping. The only ones not cheering me on were Brady, Dylan, Mason, Logan, and Cody. The five stooges sat with their arms crossed, scowling. I took a deep breath and left the podium on slightly less shaky legs.

Back in my seat, I looked down at the paper clutched in my hand. I was proud of myself. I came out from behind the protective wall

I'd built around myself and stood up to Brady and his friends. This moment signified the beginning of putting a crack in my armor. It was scary and exhilarating at the same time.

I sat listening to the rest of my classmates. I snorted out loud when Brady read my "Courage" poem. Miss Thomas gave me a strange look, but I just smiled back. Our writer's café went on through science class and finished just five minutes before the final bell.

Miss Thomas thanked the parents and guests for attending. My mom came over to where I was stacking the chairs.

"I'll wait for you outside, Hannah, and give you a ride home," she offered, still with a funny look on her face.

"Sure. I just have to wait for the bell and I'll be right out." She moved to the door and my eyes followed her until she disappeared down the hallway.

"That was weird," I said to myself, and jumped when Chip replied, "What's weird?"

"My mom. She's going to wait out front to give me a ride home."

"Moms giving rides is weird? My mom's giving me a ride home. I think that's pretty normal."

"First, my mom doesn't usually come to these things," and I gave him a pointed look, to which he responded with that sheepish shrug, "and second, she never waits to give me a ride home. She usually goes back to work."

"Maybe she's really proud of you and wants to tell you that," he speculated.

"Maybe," I answered, not really sure what to think.

I noticed Trudy standing by the window, arms crossed on her chest protectively, looking down at the parking lot. Her poem today was about all the great lessons that she learned from her grandma. Her grandma passed away this year and it was obvious that writing and reading her poem brought up some sad memories for her. I walked over, but didn't say anything. After a moment she realized that I was standing there and looked at me warily.

I smiled. "I liked your poem. It reminded me of my Grandma Eve and all the things I love doing with her. It sounds like your grandma was an awesome lady."

She mumbled her thanks and smiled in return.

Miss Thomas dismissed us at the bell. My mom was waiting in her car in front of the school chatting with Shelley, who was standing beside our car. I opened the passenger door and climbed in.

"We'll talk soon, Shelley. Take care of that boy," Mom said, nodding toward Chip, now standing next to his mom. We both waved goodbye and pulled out onto the street.

It was quiet in the car as we turned down Maple Street.

"It's early yet, Hannah. Why don't we go to the Milky Way and get some ice cream before we have to go home and make supper?" Mom suggested.

My mom taking me for ice cream—before supper? I wasn't going to argue. I replied, trying to hide the happy surprise in my voice, "Sure!"

After we got our ice cream from George (mine was Tiger Tiger, of course, and my mom had boring old vanilla), we found a table and sat down. I was enjoying my ice cream when my mom cleared her throat. I looked at her. She was smiling nervously.

"So, Hannah," she started, "your poem … is that how you really feel, like you're invisible?"

How did I explain to my mother that for a major portion of my life I felt invisible without hurting her feelings? I quietly gathered my thoughts.

"Hannah?" she prompted.

"Look, Mom," I began, "school is tough, you know?"

"Yes, Hannah. I went to school, too. I know it's tough. But trying to be invisible isn't the answer," she said, slipping right back in to lecture mode.

"Sometimes it's just easier, Mom. Kids can be cruel. So if you stay under the radar, there's less chance you get hurt," I explained.

"I get that, but you have to know that you can't mask who you are. You have talents and gifts that no one else has, as you showed today. You can't hide that. It's who you are. Be proud of it. I know your dad and I are," she said, and I was surprised by her praise. That was new.

I tried to digest what my mom just said. I didn't ever remember her telling me she was proud of me. I started to choke up. I looked out my window at the people walking down the street.

"Thanks, Mom," I finally managed without my voice breaking.

She glanced at me and replied with a smile, "You're welcome."

After ice cream we stopped at the McNevins' store to pick up some groceries for supper. When we turned the last corner to our house, I sat up straighter in the seat and all the good feelings I'd felt a minute before were gone, replaced with a dark feeling of dread.

Parked in front of our house was a police car.

I knew the shock I felt was written all over my face. It was the same look I saw mirrored on Mom's, her eyes big and eyebrows raised. We looked at each other for a moment and as she passed the police car and slowly pulled into our driveway I got a second shock.

Trudy, and a woman who had to be her mother because they were mirror images of each other, stood on our front step talking to my father and two police officers.

My mom and I got out of the car and climbed the steps.

"Angie," Mom nodded to Trudy's mom, who nodded back.

"Mike," my mom asked, "what's going on?"

"The police are here, along with Trudy and her mother, because Trudy has given a statement to the police about Chip's beating," Dad answered.

I turned my surprised gaze to Trudy. She had evidence about who beat up Chip? Questions raced through my mind.

Before I could ask anything, however, one of the officers spoke, reading from the little notebook in his hand. "Apparently, Trudy overheard Brady Robinson bragging to some students at the baseball game, two days ago, about how he had finally taught Toby Cavanagh a lesson. He named his accomplices and the extent of Toby's injuries and how they had repeatedly punched and kicked him in the stomach, face, and arms."

"So what's going to happen now?" my mom asked.

"Based on what Trudy's told us, I think we have enough evidence to press charges against all the boys involved. I would, however, like to talk to Hannah and make sure that we have the details right about when and where she left Toby, to corroborate what Trudy has told us."

When I looked at Trudy again, she was smiling. "You're not the only one who wants to be seen for who they really are," she whispered.

I jerked my head back at her comment, then smiled myself.

I gave the police my details of the walk home on the night Chip was beaten, and they left, I assumed to go and arrest Brady and his friends.

Trudy and her mom left right after. As they walked to their car, my mom and dad went into the house. I stood in the doorway, and when Trudy looked at me through the window of the car I gave a small wave. She returned it.

I closed the door and looked in the living room. My dad was sitting in his chair with the news on, as always. I walked to the kitchen to find my mom gathering ingredients for supper. I stood beside her at the kitchen counter.

"Anything I can help with?" I asked.

She wrapped her arm around my shoulder.

"I'm proud of you, Hannah," she said, and hugged me to her. I wrapped my arms around her waist and hugged her back.

In the reflection of the patio doors I saw my mom and I. Not just my mom. But my mom and I. I was no longer invisible. I saw … me.

"I think I am, too," I said, smiling.

ACKNOWLEDGMENTS

When you think of an author, what image comes to mind? Do you imagine a solitary person creating behind closed doors? Nothing could be further from the truth. While the acting of writing is a solitary endeavour, a number of people have played a monumental role in helping me bring this book to you.

I owe a huge "thank you" to the following people, without whom this story would not have made it to the page:

To R.E. Vance, who taught me more about writing a novel in three hours than I ever learned in school.

To the Nerdy Wordsmith, Spencer Hamilton, editor extraordinaire, who took my novel, made it better and provided a wealth of constructive feedback.

To Gayle Dos Anjos, my accountabillabuddy, for the support and encouragement and helping me stay on track!

To Rob Westerburg, coach and techie genius, who has stood beside me as I went down the path of becoming an author. For the encouragement, the belief, and the gentle nudges that sometimes became pushes, there are not enough thank yous! While you take little credit for this, I am certain it wouldn't have happened without you!

To my family and friends who have been so supportive, encouraging and excited about this novel, you have overwhelmed me time and again. You are amazing!

To my husband Terry, who cooked meals, bought groceries and did laundry while I wrote—you win Husband of the Year!

Finally, I must thank you, the reader, for picking up this book and taking the time to get to know Hannah and Chip. It was created for you!

AUTHOR BIO

See Me is the debut novel of H.R. Hobbs. An educator for nearly thirty years, she began teaching with the goal of sharing her love of books with her students. A mother to three grown sons and grandmother to two little darlings, she resides with her husband in the small prairie town where she was born and raised. You can find her online at www.hrhobbsbooks.ca.

Made in the USA
Charleston, SC
14 November 2016